Today was Monday. That meant I had only tomorrow before the news about Gillian Dawn and the movie being made at the Beaumont mansion was common knowledge. What could I do in that one solitary day to turn this incredible stroke of luck into my golden opportunity?

I would go to the Beaumont mansion tomorrow. *How*, I hadn't figured out yet. And I would get onto the set and meet Gillian Dawn. I hadn't mapped that out yet, either. And when we met, I would so dazzle her with my star quality that she would beg me to come out to the coast.

SHEILA HAYES is the author of several books for young people. She and her husband have three daughters, and live in Briarcliff Manor, New York.

NO AUTOGRAPHS, PLEASE

SHEILA HAYES

Pacer BOOKS FOR YOUNG ADULTS

BERKLEY BOOKS, NEW YORK

for my brother, Jim,
who knows all the old movies

1

It was dawn in Camelot. The rustling of the leaves underfoot seemed like a chorus of appreciative sighs as Queen Guinevere (played by Cynthia Star) tripped lightly through the forest. Even the tiny woodland creatures scurried about in excitement as she passed. As she stooped to gather a bouquet, the grace of her movements flooding the screen with beauty, the camera moved in to get a close-up of that face adored by millions. Suddenly the sound of hoofbeats could be heard in the distance. Guinevere straightened, a look of concern clouding her perfect features. Then she turned, and her face brightened as Lancelot (played by Timothy Hutton) leapt from his horse and fell to his knees at her feet. As the background music swelled to a crescendo, he raised his eyes and gazed at her for a long moment. Finally he spoke.

"You gonna eat the rest of that sandwich?"

Benny Krupchik was leaning over me, ready to pounce on the uneaten half of my ham on rye. As usual, he had wolfed down his own lunch and was ready to devour whatever he could of everybody else's.

"Yes, I am," I said, hurriedly taking a bite before he could grab it out of my hand.

"What have you been staring at?" Nancy asked.

"What do you mean?"

"What d'you mean, *what do I mean?* You've been staring out the window for the last five minutes as if you never saw trees before."

"I was just drinking in their beauty," I said.

Nancy rolled her eyes. "I don't know how you get away with it, Starrett. I was watching you in English this morning. You drink in any more beauty, and you're gonna flunk for sure."

"Why should I flunk? I'm not stupid, you know. Just because I don't find school as thrilling as you do."

"Cut it out! I don't find it thrilling, and you know it. When I see those autumn leaves, all it reminds me of is that we're starting another whole year of school. But I'd get killed if I brought home C's."

When the subject of grades came up, I usually changed the subject. And when Nancy tried to make me feel like a dummy, I usually tried to get even.

"I thought you were on a diet," I said as I watched her stuff a second Devil Dog into her mouth.

"Tuesday. I always start my diets on Tuesdays. In months that end with an *r*," she said, giggling.

I made a face to show her how gross I thought the whole performance was. Mom says Nancy and I fight so much we really ought to be sisters, instead of just best friends.

"Oh, come on, don't be such a grouch," she said. "You're getting into one of your moods, I can tell. Just because you didn't get the part again. What's the big deal?"

"For someone who intends to deliver piglets for a living, I guess it's not such a big deal. But *I* am an actress. And how can I be an actress, if they won't let me act?"

"Look, I know you're upset, but I'd really appreciate it if you wouldn't refer to my future career as 'delivering piglets for a living,' okay?"

"Okay," I mumbled.

"And I still don't understand why you enjoy banging your head against the wall. I told you they wouldn't let an eighth grader play Guinevere in *Camelot*."

"I said okay," I repeated. I try not to take my bad moods out on Nancy. I know you're not supposed to use your best friend for a dart board. Maybe I'm just jealous. A veterinarian is such a nice, normal thing to be. That's typical of Nancy. She's always doing nice, normal things . . . things that make her sweat and get tired and dirty.

Sometimes I wish I didn't know I was meant for a higher destiny. It gets kind of lonely just standing around, staying clean, and waiting to be discovered.

When I first started auditioning, it was fun. I think I was tougher then. When they needed twelve tap dancers for the fifth-grade musical, and fourteen of us tried out, and I was one of the two who didn't make it, I blamed it on my shoes. And when Mrs. Fitch, the chorus director, asked me please just to mouth the words to some of the songs in the annual spring concert, I tried not to take it personally.

But it's been going on for a few years now, and it's beginning to get to me. Grandma says that all I need is a stroke of luck. She says that luck is more important than talent, but I'm not so sure.

"Hey," Nancy said, draining the last of her Coke, "why don't you stay after school with the rest of us and do something nice and normal for a change? We're trying out for cheerleaders!"

See what I mean?

"No thanks," I said.

After school I walked the two blocks from the bus stop very slowly. I pass the houses on Robert Street every day, and I never bother to look at them. Usually Nancy's walking with me, and we're too busy talking to notice anything. But today, of course, she was trying out for the cheerleading squad. I just couldn't explain to her that I don't want to cheer people on—I want to be the one they're cheering on. I get so afraid sometimes that I'm going to be just an ordinary person all my life and never do anything special. I think I'll die if that happens. Maybe it's a flaw in my character, something I was born with. But to tell the truth, I think it all began with that fortune-teller.

It happened the summer I was nine years old. There was a carnival in the next town, and Grandma took me over to see it. After we had gone on some of the rides, we stopped at this fortune-teller's booth. It cost $2.50 (I thought that was where the fortune came in), but Grandma believes in that sort of thing, and she wanted me to have my fortune told. I remember the woman very clearly: She had a mane of auburn hair, huge silver hoops dangled from her earlobes, and she wore so much powdery white makeup that the wrinkles in her face stood out like ski tracks on a mountain slope.

Anyway, what she said was—are you ready?—she told us that one day I would be very famous. My picture would be on a magazine cover, and everybody all over the world would know who I was. And as if that wasn't enough, she topped it by saying this would all come about, at least in part, because of my great beauty. Can you imagine? Talk about a crystal ball! I mean, the other day I looked at my fourth-grade class picture, and I looked like a mongoose.

But as I said, Grandma believes in these things, and she took the prediction to mean only one thing: I would follow in her footsteps and become an actress. Better than just an actress, I'd be a STAR. (Also, being in her own weird way a very down-to-earth sort of person, Grandma mulled it over for a week and, using her own particular process of elimination, decided it would not be *Time, Newsweek,* or *Sports Illustrated.* The magazine cover I was fated to grace was *People.*)

That made it even more real and tangible to me, because Grandma should know, shouldn't she? She almost made it herself. She went to Hollywood when she was young and made three movies. Even though she was just an extra—I mean she didn't have any lines to say—she could be seen. And if she hadn't met Grandpa, she might have made it all the way to the top. He was a grip—that's one of the workers on a movie set—and when they fell in love and got married, they moved back East and settled down. But they stayed in show business. They opened the Star, which until a few years ago was the only movie theatre in Schuyler. It's still a beautiful theatre, much bigger than the new Cinema 21 they opened on the other side of town. That one's so long and skinny it feels like you're sitting in a bowling alley. The Star has golden cherubs gazing down on Burt Reynolds as he struts across the screen, and a sweep of ruby velvet on either side of the stage. The seats are a little worn now, but to me it's still a palace.

My grandfather died ten years ago, but Dad took over and now he manages the Star for Grandma, even though he and Mom aren't at all like Gram and me.

Anyway, today as I walked home, I took the time to look at all the houses on my block. They were lined up in a row as if they were just waiting to be inspected. They're identical, except that each one is painted a different color. I think if you saw my block from an airplane, it would look like a picture out of a coloring book: one house red, one house yellow, one house green. The green one was our house, number 35, but I sailed on by. No one would be home yet. Mom doesn't get home from Crandall's until six, and Walter was at Mrs. Mueller's for his piano lesson. I passed the Prescotts'. They had put on new green shutters, I noticed. Their house is white, so it looked really nice. The stone cat on the Reillys' roof had lost a front paw over the summer, and the Willoughbys had put out two pots of flaming red mums to celebrate autumn.

I turned in at the shingled yellow house with the neat 49 on the mailbox. Grandma never locked her door, so I went right in, and there she was, scraping a carrot at the kitchen sink. She stood as tall and straight as a soldier on sentry duty. People say she looks like Katherine Hepburn, but I don't think so. I think she looks like those statues you see in churches and fancy art books. Her face is chiseled and fine, with beautiful bones, and even though I know she must be pretty old now, she never seems that way to me. She has an air of adventure about her that I've always loved—as if at any moment she'll throw a cape over her shoulders and rush out the door, jump on her horse, and gallop off on some great, mysterious errand.

Today, as she stood there peeling vegetables, she wore a spangled, glittering dress that barely reached to her knees. It was the color of silver, and it had tassels—the kind you see on old-fashioned drapes—all over the hem. It was her flapper costume, the one she wore in *Roaring Twenties*. Over it, she had tossed a dark red cardigan.

"Gram?" I called, hating to interrupt her because she had that dreamy look about her as if she were a million miles away. She gets that way sometimes. "Sorry, luv," she'll say, "my body was here, but my mind was in California, the time I almost had a screen test for Scarlett O'Hara . . ." or "Did you say somethin', Cynthia? I'm afraid I was in London just now with my sister, Mildred, the summer we were twenty-one."

"Gram?" I repeated softly.

"Hmm?" She turned, and then seeing me, she broke into a big smile. "Cyn-thi-a! How nice to see you!"

Then, turning off the water and drying her hands on a towel, she said, "Come here and give me a hug!"

I did, and then I helped myself to some peanut butter and bread and made myself a sandwich.

"So what's new, luv?" she asked, busying herself with her dinner preparations. Grandma always eats early, so her dinner's usually on the stove by three o'clock.

I made a face. "Don't ask," I said, with an exaggerated sigh.

She turned from the counter and looked at me. Then she said, as if she had just remembered something important, "Oh, was it today? The audition! It was today . . . oh dear." Her voice trailed off as she looked at my face. "Sweetie, don't you feel one bit bad. It happens. It happens. I came this close to gettin' a part I can't tell you how many times. It coulda been the color of your hair—was she dark, the one who got it? You've got that gorgeous golden hair, luv, but if they wanted a dark, exotic type. . . . Or your height. That was it, I'll bet. You're tall, like all the Starretts, let's face it. I bet whoever got it was a midget, am I right?"

I couldn't help laughing, and I went over and gave her another hug. "No, she wasn't a midget, Grandma. She was a twelfth grader, that's what she was. I could have tried out for one of the ladies-in-waiting, but a lot of good that's gonna do me."

"Just you hang in there, Cynthia. Like I always told you, you're destiny's child. Remember that. Somethin'll happen soon."

"I know, Gram," I said, wandering into what Grandma calls the parlor, with my peanut butter sandwich in one hand and a glass of milk in the other. That's one of the things I like best about Grandma's. I could never take peanut butter into my mother's living room. Our house has to stay neat-as-a-pin. When Mom's not working at Crandall's measuring out bolts of cloth, she likes nothing more than being down on her knees with a pail and a sponge. It's kind of like living in an operating room. Grandma says my mom is compensating because my dad likes playing around with cars and coming home covered with grease. He works down at Jerry's Garage on Saturdays. Most of the time, my dad's the real silent type. But on Saturdays he comes home whistling.

Did I mention that my dad's name is Walter? He was Grandma's only child, and she named him after her favorite actor, Walter Pidgeon. I asked her one time, "Didn't Grandpa mind naming his son after someone else?" but she said "No, 'cause he was Grandpa's favorite actor, too." It has one advantage. My kid brother's name is Walter, Jr., and whenever he's being a brat (which is about 99 percent of the time), I get him good with "At least they didn't name *me* after a pigeon!" You can see the kind of close-knit family we are.

Grandma followed me into the parlor and settled herself in her favorite chair after shooing Snowball off. The cat leapt onto the floor in a great cloud of white fur.

"You've rearranged the pictures," I said. The round table in the corner was covered with photographs of all sizes: pictures of Walter and me as babies, pictures of my dad when he was little, pictures of Grandpa. But my favorites were the kind that no other family had. Pictures of Grandma when she was young, with her face framed by a circle of blonde curls, and her big blue eyes staring off into the distance like she was looking straight into heaven. Those were pictures from her portfolio. Her professional pictures.

"Yep. I did some cleanin' today," she said, with an air of self-satisfaction.

"I figured," I said, laughing and nodding at her outfit.

She laughed back and smoothed the silver tassels, trying to stretch them so they'd cover her knees. Grandma was so different from Mom. Grandma hated to clean, so when she had to, she'd put on something that made her feel good. Housework was dull enough, she said. Why do it in a shapeless old sack that made it more of a chore? It made sense to me.

I looked at the old-fashioned clock on the fireplace. "I've gotta go," I said. "Walter'll be getting home soon."

Grandma got up and walked me to the door. "So long, luv. Thanks for stoppin' by. And remember what I said: Somethin'll happen soon. I know it will!"

"I know it will too, Gram," I said, trying to sound like I meant it.

I slung my knapsack over my shoulder and headed home, never suspecting that while I was rekindling the fires of my ambition with a peanut butter sandwich, fate was already altering the path my fortunes were to take. Grandma was right. Something would happen soon.

What happened was Gillian Dawn.

2

It always amazes me the kind of messenger fate picks for this sort of thing. For the earthshaking news that Gillian Dawn had arrived in town, news that would alter my world forever, the gods chose Benny Krupchik.

It was a glorious afternoon, and the big oak tree out in back of the school still had a full canopy of leaves. Lying under it now was like looking up into a green-and-gold forest. I could almost be Guinevere again, except that now, having lost the part, that daydream was losing its appeal. I stretched out, totally relaxed, and listened to the conversation going on around me.

Nancy was reciting the rigors of cheerleading practice as if she weren't absolutely thrilled to have made the squad. When we were younger, Nancy was on the pudgy side, and she was always the last chosen for any games we played at recess. But she had slimmed down recently, and I knew the thought of twirling around in her short little cheerleading skirt had her in orbit.

"I think they're trying to kill us," she was saying. "I swear, our workouts are tougher than the football team's."

"No way," Petey Gonzalez said. "Man, you don't know what you're talking about. You'd break in two if you had to work out with us for five minutes."

There was a chorus of grunts that I took to mean that the boys around the tree outnumbered the girls and were ganging up on poor Nance. But the conversation was boring.

The stadium was bursting with the screams of a thousand cheering fans. There were only fourteen seconds left to play in the championship game, and the score was tied. Cynthia Star, as Penny Doolittle, captain of the cheerleaders, was performing to the delight and amazement of the thunderous crowd. Quarterback Greg Strong (played by Timothy Hutton) looked over to her for encouragement. One smile from her was all that he needed. Music swelled in the background as the cameras caught the panorama of pennants and pom-poms and whistle-blowing and speakers blaring. Greg mouthed some words in Penny's direction, but she couldn't hear him over the din of the crowd. She tried to read his lips, and the camera zoomed in for a close-up. He seemed to be saying—

"You got a quarter on you?"
"Huh?"
"Where were you, half-asleep?" Nancy asked.

"Uh, no. I was just thinking of all the homework I've got tonight."

"Don't remind me. Well, do you or don't you?"

"What?"

"Have a quarter?"

"Oh. Uh-uh. I'm broke. I mean flat."

"Shoot. I'm still starving."

"Hey, you guys, did I tell you who moved into town over the weekend?"

It was Benny Krupchik talking. Benny is a regular little old lady when it comes to gossip. His dad works for the Schuyler *Gazette*, and Benny always hears about things before the rest of us.

"No, who moved into town over the weekend?" somebody asked, grabbing the bait.

"How much is it worth?"

"Oh, come on Benny, stop acting like a jerk."

"Yeah, we're not gonna pay you for some dumb bit of news that'll be in the paper tonight."

"This won't be in the paper tonight. Not yet. It's real confidential."

"Well, if it's not gonna be in the paper it can't be that important," Mark said.

"It would be to some people," Benny said, nudging my sneaker with his foot.

I sat up and looked at him, picking bits of leaves out of my hair as I did. "Me? Why would it be important to me?"

"Because she wants to be a movie star when she grows up," Benny said, in a little-girl voice that sent the others into peals of laughter. I could feel my face getting red.

"C'mon you guys, lay off Cici. You're just jealous," Nancy said.

"Yeah, Cici," Jody added, "when you're famous, don't give them your autograph."

I had been afraid of this ever since I admitted my "secret" ambition at Jody's birthday party last year. I grinned to show what a good sport I was.

"That's right," I said, waving them away. "Whenever you guys show up, it'll be, 'No autographs, please.' "

"Okay Benny, we can't stand it anymore. Who is it?" Mark asked.

Benny waited a moment till he had our attention. Then he popped a couple of jelly beans in his mouth and waited while he chewed and swallowed each one.

"Ben-ny," Nancy said. "If it's not somebody absolutely fantastic, you realize we're gonna kill you."

"Gillian Dawn," he said, the words popping out of his mouth as smoothly and quickly as the jelly beans had just popped in.

"Gillian Dawn," Mark repeated, adding, "the movie star?"

Benny nodded, pleased with the reception his news had received.

I didn't say anything. I was too stunned. Even though we live only forty minutes from New York City, the closest I ever got to a celebrity was last Christmastime, on Fifth Avenue and 57th Street. And then it was Warner Wolf, the sportscaster for Channel 2.

Suddenly we were all talking at once.

"How'd you find out?"

"Where is she staying?"

"Why'd she come here?"

"Are you sure?"

"One at a time, please," Benny said, obviously savoring his moment of power. This was almost as good as the time the police had the names of the people who were selling drugs to kids in Beaumont Park. Two "prominent" citizens were involved, and the town buzzed for days about who they were. Benny's father knew, and Benny pretended he did, too, but we never believed him. They turned out to be a guy who worked in the drugstore and a bank teller who was a deacon in Nancy's church. That was by far the best news story Schuyler ever had. We even had a camera crew here from CBS News.

"Okay, Benny," I said, "but tell us . . . what's she doing here?"

"Well now, nobody is supposed to know this—so don't tell anyone or I'll get murdered—but she's here to make a movie."

"A movie!" we all screeched.

"This is so exciting, I can't stand it," Jody said. Then she poked me so hard I thought she broke a rib. "You must be dying!"

In truth, I was suspended somewhere beyond dying. It was happening, I knew it. And knowing—the pure certainty that my destiny was at hand—calmed me down. I sat with my legs crossed under me, yoga-fashion, like someone in meditation, listening to everyone babbling around me.

"What's the name of the movie?" someone asked.

"*The House With a Thousand Eyes*. It's one of those

scary comedies, and they're shooting it in the old Beaumont mansion."

"I can't stand it!" Jody squealed again. I had never seen her so excited. "Who else is in it? Any cute guys?"

Benny shook his head. "I dunno."

"Where is she gonna live?"

"She's rented a place over on the Hudson. One of those big modern jobs."

"But why isn't anyone supposed to know?"

"They will. My dad said the lack of publicity is supposed to get them publicity. They're going to have stuff in the paper about how she won't give any interviews, and how spooky the movie is. That kind of crap. The set's gonna be closed."

The last bit caught my attention. So far I hadn't had to expose myself to any more ribbing by asking any questions, because all the others were asking them for me. Now I ventured a small one.

"How do you know the set is going to be closed?"

"Because that's what it said in the press kit my dad has. I wasn't supposed to look at it, but I always do anyway," he said.

"So when is it going to be in the papers?" Mark asked.

"Wednesday. After that, Dad said, the Beaumont place will be crawling with sightseers and autograph hounds."

And after that, my chance of being discovered by Gillian Dawn would go down to zero.

In the midst of everyone talking, we heard the bell that signaled the end of lunch hour. We had three minutes to get to class. As we surged toward the doors, Nancy came up behind me and grabbed my arm.

"I bet you're flying," she said.

I shrugged my shoulders to show how nonchalant I was. "It's probably more exciting for people who have no other contact with show business," I said, nodding in Jody's direction.

Why I say things like that, I'll never know. And why I say them to Nancy, who knows me so well, is even more of a mystery.

"I think you've finally snapped, Starrett," she said, and with that she let go of my arm and headed for the art room. I had English next, and I feel honor bound to confess that I never heard a word, not one word, that Miss Scott said.

When I got home, I made a beeline for the bathroom mirror. But, of course, there was no change. The face that looked out at me was the same face that had looked out at me this morning. Which was where this whole thing got to be depressing. I believe in fate. I believe in luck. I believe that Gillian Dawn was an angel, a shimmering, golden-haired angel sent by the gods to lead me up to that pantheon where those special mortals reside who are possessed with great intellect, talent, or beauty.

There had to be a reason why I was getting my big break before I was even passably attractive, never mind a great beauty. I mean, the gods don't mess up, do they?

Today was Monday. That meant I had only tomorrow before the news about Gillian Dawn and the movie being made at the Beaumont mansion was common knowledge. What could I do in that one solitary day to turn this incredible stroke of luck into my golden opportunity?

I would go to the Beaumont mansion tomorrow. *How*, I hadn't figured out yet. Grandma would think of something. And I would get onto the set and meet Gillian Dawn. I hadn't mapped that out yet, either. And when we met, I would so dazzle her with my star quality that she would beg me to come out to the coast.

Los Angeles, November 8th . . . Gillian Dawn, reigning cinema queen, is busy telling everyone who'll listen about an exciting discovery. While shooting her new movie, The House With a Thousand Eyes, in the tiny Hudson hamlet of Schuyler, New York, she happened upon a young talent by the name of Cynthia Star. "She looks like Brooke Shields, and she acts like a dream," Miss Dawn told this reporter. Several contracts have been dangled under the young lady's nose, but Miss Star intends to finish out the eighth grade at Schuyler Central. Hopes are she'll squeeze in a movie debut during her summer vacation.

I already had the height, I consoled myself, *and* the bushy eyebrows. But by tomorrow afternoon, the rest of me had to look like Brooke Shields, too.

Or maybe even better.

3

The huge black gates towered over me menacingly. I had made it this far, but I didn't have the faintest idea how I was going to get beyond these gates and onto the set. I shifted my weight from one foot to another, but the knapsack on my back seemed to be loaded with rocks. It was one of those days that we had so much homework, I had to bring home almost every book from my locker.

As I stared at the great stone pillars and the overgrown path that disappeared into the woods beyond, I felt like someone in a gothic novel. The heroine of *Rebecca*, gazing at Manderley for the first time. But I had the feeling that the knapsack made me look more like a refugee from *The Sound of Music*. I slipped it off my back and let it fall to the side of the road. Then I sat down on a rock to think for a moment.

It had been surprisingly easy to get this far. Grandma and I both decided that I should come by myself.

Much as she would have loved to drive me over, to steal onto the set herself, we knew my chances of being "discovered" were better if I just accidentally happened by. It was Grandma who remembered that I had baby-sat a few times for the Greenleafs, who live two blocks from the mansion. That's what I told Nancy: I was taking the number 8 bus because I had a baby-sitting job. She didn't know the Greenleafs, so she couldn't catch me in a lie. And I would call Grandma from the gas station down the road when I needed a lift home.

But what was I supposed to do between now and that golden moment when I start down the road, movie contract in my pocket, yodeling happily? I stared down at the ground as if the answer lay buried in the dirt. Then I rummaged in my knapsack and found the tools that I had squirreled away before I left home this morning. I took the barrettes out of my hair and gave it a good brushing. Since my long blonde hair is my sole physical asset, I let it hang loose and (I hoped) beautifully untamed over my shoulders. Then I took out the blusher and looked in the mirror. I was sure I didn't have all those pimples on my chin when I left the house this morning.

Why was I doing this? It was hopeless. Lip gloss, that would help! I should have worn real makeup . . . tons of it. I bet Brooke wouldn't look so good if her mother went catatonic every time she tried a little eye shadow.

I stood up and went over to the gates again and peered in, but the road just wandered off into woods and trees and silence. I had never seen the Beaumont mansion. It had been deserted for years, and until now I had never cared about it, but I could feel its presence surrounding me today.

The setting lent itself to a period drama.

I would be wearing a long old-fashioned gown made of green velvet, and a cape with a hood. I'd present a haunting picture, gazing in at the estate, while behind me there would come the clatter of hoofbeats, and a young nobleman (played by Timothy Hutton) would jump off his horse, fall to his knees, and ask reverently—

"What're you staring at?"

I whirled around, and as usual, reality came crashing down around me with a thud. It was a boy about my age. He was a little shorter than me, and he was looking at me like he had never seen a human before. I couldn't seem to speak, and he didn't speak again either, so we just stood there eyeing each other in silence.

Finally he repeated, "What're you staring at?"

I shook my head and that seemed to free me from the zombielike trance I had stumbled into. "I wasn't staring at anything," I said. "I just stopped for a moment."

"No one's allowed in there, so you'd better scram."

"I don't have to scram," I said indignantly. "This is public property. This is . . . this is . . ."—I looked at the winding country lane—"this is a public highway."

To my surprise, he started to laugh. I began to relax. When he had just stood there staring at me, it had made me kind of nervous. While his laughing made *me* a little less nervous, it didn't, in truth, do much for him. He had braces on his teeth.

"Egads . . . this *is* the sticks! You call this a highway?"

"I didn't mean that. You just got me confused. And it's not the sticks. This is New York."

"Well, it sure ain't the Big Apple. What'd you say your name was?"

"I didn't tell you my name."

"Well, are you going to? You're trespassing, you know."

"I am not!"

"You are too. This property out here belongs to the Beaumont Trust. That means you're trespassing. You could get in a lot of trouble if I wanted to be mean and report you." I tried to look unconcerned, but the thought of my presence outside the Beaumont gates being known around town made me shudder. "But I won't," he went on, "if you go right now. Honest, I've been told to report anybody that hangs around out here."

I picked up my knapsack and adjusted it on my back. It wasn't going exactly as I had planned. Part of me was ready to burst into tears of disappointment and frustration, but part of me was thinking: Get your tail out of here before you get into real trouble! A third part of me opened my mouth and said, "All right, but I wouldn't want to be in your shoes when Gillian hears about this!"

"What?"

I had caught his interest.

"Miss Dawn. I just stopped by to say hello, and

she's not going to like you being so rude to a . . . a friend of her daughter's."

She did have a daughter, I was sure of it. But how old? Or was it a son? Or maybe just a dog? I started to leave.

"Wait! Wait a minute. Did you say you know her daughter?"

I paused to savor the new note of respect in his voice. I nodded.

He looked puzzled and a little hesitant. "How come you know Judy?"

My gamble had worked. "Uh . . . we met one time when she was in New York. When she knew her mother was coming here to shoot the movie, she told me to be sure and stop by and say hello." He didn't look entirely convinced. "How else could I have known about the movie being shot in there?"

That did it.

"You're right," he said, seeming to relax and believe me for the first time. "So you're a friend of Judy's!"

I nodded. Then a horrible thought hit me. "Uh, she's not here now, is she?"

"No, no, she's not," he said quickly. "But come on, I'll take you inside. There's a back way that's left open for the crew. I'll take you to see Miss Dawn myself."

I stood there for a moment, unable to move. Then (unbidden by me, I swear to it), my feet began to follow this strange errand boy. We went down the road a bit, and then up a steep path that cut through what looked like dense thicket. A way had been cleared there, whether many years ago or just recently, I couldn't be sure.

The thought occurred to me that I was crazy to follow this perfect stranger. What if he attacked me? I slipped my knapsack off my shoulders and held it at my side, ready to use as a weapon. For the first time that day, I was delighted that it felt as if it were loaded with bowling balls.

"Do you work here?" I said, panting as I struggled to keep up with him.

"I came with the crew. My mom works on the set, and I do odd jobs." He stopped for a moment so I stopped, too. "By the way," he said "you never did tell me your name."

"Cynthia. Cynthia Starrett. But my friends call me Cici. What's yours?"

"Homer Montague."

I thought I hadn't heard him correctly. "Homer . . . your name is *Homer*?" I repeated.

He nodded.

I tried to think of something nice to say. "What do your friends call you?" I asked.

"Homer," he said.

We started walking again, and suddenly I could see some men moving around in the distance. One was talking into a walkie-talkie, another was making notes on a clipboard. There was equipment everywhere: trucks loaded with gear, cameras, sound booms, wire strung through the trees, and campers, their doors flying open and shut as people hurried in and out. What had looked like a wilderness was a city. And in the center, looking like a stone wallflower at the ball, sat the Beaumont mansion.

It wasn't really that big, but it had pillars in the front, which made it look very impressive; and there was ivy crawling up the walls and completely covering some of the windows, which made it look very spooky. Maybe it had been white at one time, but now it was a dingy gray. It looked sorry and lonely and deserted—exactly the way a haunted house ought to look.

Homer turned to me and held a finger up to his lips. Then he motioned me to sit on the ground next to him and not move. One of the men—I assumed he was the director—was barking orders through a loudspeaker. Then the set was still, and I knew they were filming because a camera was moving back and forth in front of the mansion silently. But nothing seemed to be happening. Then from out of the woods, an old-fashioned black car drove up to the front door and stopped. A small woman with long blonde hair that tumbled from under a big floppy hat stepped out from the driver's seat. It was Gillian Dawn. Without realizing I was doing it, I punched my companion. He turned angrily, and I had to pantomime an apology. Was he so used to this that he didn't get excited?

She had gone up to the front door and was fumbling with a key when the director called "Cut."

Homer let out a sigh of relief. Or was it boredom? Or was he just holding his breath? Then, as if he had just remembered I was there, he turned.

"When was the last time you saw Judy?"

"Oh, uh, last year."

"She's pretty, don't you think?" he said.

"Oh yeah. Beautiful."

"Her hair especially." He tried to look wicked. "I go for blondes," he said.

I was beginning to get the picture. This poor thing

had a crush on the star's daughter! How sad. She probably didn't even know he existed.

"By the way," he said, "I'm sorry I came on so strong back there. But the director asked me to keep the neighborhood kids away."

"Oh, that's okay. Where's your mother?" I asked, looking around the set. Everyone seemed to have disappeared into campers.

"She's in one of those dressing rooms," he said.

"Maybe I'd better go," I said, after we had sat for a moment in silence.

"No, no, wait a minute. I think they're finished for the day. Wait here."

He got up and crossed the set with the easy assurance of one who belonged there. How wonderful his life must be, I thought. Maybe his mother was Miss Dawn's hairdresser. Maybe she was the wardrobe mistress. . . .

He disappeared into one of the campers and reappeared about ten minutes later. He looked across at me and waved me over.

I got up slowly. I couldn't walk across the intricate web of wires and cables so nonchalantly. I felt myself trembling. What was I doing here? Why wasn't I more dressed up? Could I duck behind a tree for a minute and brush my hair again? But he met me halfway.

"C'mon," he said, "Miss Dawn wants to meet you."

My heart was pounding so loudly, I was sure the sound man was picking it up on his mike. We went up two steps and into a camper that was much bigger than it looked from the outside. Gillian Dawn was sitting in an armchair reading her script. She was wearing a purple satin robe and had a cigarette in one hand and a mug of coffee in the other. A golden retriever got up from the pink shag rug and barked at me unconvincingly. Then it went back and lay down by the chair.

Two other people were in the room—a woman who was arranging some dresses on a rack, and the man I had identified as the director.

Gillian Dawn looked up and smiled at us. "Well, Homer, introduce me to your friend."

I moved a little closer. She was pretty, even with all the makeup she had to wear, which showed up the little lines around her eyes and at the corners of her mouth. Her eyes were almond-shaped and dark, just like in her pictures, and her hair was golden blonde and hung loosely around her shoulders.

"This is," he hesitated a moment, looking at me.

"Cynthia Starrett," I said shakily.

He nodded and added, "She says she's a friend of your daughter, Judy."

Instead of the outstretched hand and broad smile I had expected, a puzzled frown crossed her face, and the smile vanished.

"What?"

"I said," he repeated, in what I thought was a rather rude tone of voice, "she says she's a friend of your daughter, Judy."

I began to feel very uncomfortable. How could I have done such a stupid thing. Somehow they knew I was a fraud. I began to babble, "Well, perhaps she never mentioned me. It's been a while. . . ."

I was only a few feet inside the door of the camper, but I had never felt so trapped in my life. Then, suddenly, the tension was broken by a peal of laughter.

Gillian Dawn was laughing, a high-pitched giggle that I recognized from her movies. She put her coffee cup down as it began to spill.

"Oh kid, you are the pits. What're you up to now?"

Homer shrugged and stood there looking like someone who had just scored 20,000 in Donkey Kong.

Gillian Dawn leaned over and grabbed the collar of the beautiful dog at her feet.

"Miss Whatever-your-name-is, does this look like my daughter? Meet Judy. The only Judy I know. Judy, meet—what was your name?"

I stood there, my face crimson, and whispered, "Cynthia Starrett."

She looked over her shoulder at Homer. "You're mean, kid, real mean."

I wanted to scream at her, "You can say that again, Miss Dawn!" He had to be the meanest, sneakiest, rottenest kid I'd ever met in my whole life. I had never hated anybody like I hated him at that moment. I started backing toward the door. If I could make it outside without another word, I would. I would run and run and never look back at this horrible place. But as I edged toward the doorway, Gillian Dawn looked at me, startled.

"Oh, don't leave, Cynthia! Not when Homer's gone to all this length to bring you here. Homer knows I like to meet my fans. Right, Homer?" she said, giving him a big, bright smile he didn't deserve.

"Right," he said, looking for the first time like he might be a little uncomfortable. "It was just a joke," he said to me offhandedly. "You were being such a smart ass. I'm going to get a Coke," he said, looking at me. "You want one?"

I shook my head violently, and he shrugged and ducked out the door.

When he was gone, I let out my breath slowly. I think I'd been holding it for about ten minutes.

"Miss Dawn," I began hesitantly, taking a step forward, "I want you to know I'm so sorry. I *am* your fan, your *biggest* fan. It was all his fault. I was waiting at the gate, hoping to get your autograph, and he told me to come in and he'd introduce me. He . . . he practically dragged me in here. I certainly hope he doesn't cause you trouble like this all the time!"

"Well, as a matter of fact . . ."

"Maybe you should speak to his mother," I said. "If she works for you, she should tell him not to bother you. You're such an important star!"

He poked his head in the door and gave me what was supposed to be a friendly grin. I stared back at him stonily. I'd get him good. When I was finished, I'd be in good with Gillian Dawn, and he'd be kept on a leash somewhere.

"Sorry to interrupt this little chat, but I forgot to ask"—he looked over to Gillian Dawn—"You want more coffee, Mom?"

4

What'd I do? What would *you* have done? I ran.

Unfortunately grace and agility have never been my strong points, and as I made my exit from the trailer, I forgot that there were two small steps to the ground: I stepped off into thin air and fell like a stone into the dirt.

If ever there was a time for a fade-out, this was it. Here's where fantasy really has it all over reality. If I were the heroine in a story, they'd do a quick cut to another scene or else have a long fade-out with a close-up of my anguished (but still incredibly beautiful) face, or at the very least, they'd pause for a word from the sponsor.

But here I was, as usual, stuck with real life.

As I began to get up, rubbing a sore knee with a scraped hand, I felt someone take hold of my elbow, steadying me. I whirled around to face the director.

"You okay?" he said gently. I realized I was on the

verge of tears, and not trusting myself to speak, I just nodded. "Gillie would like to see you back inside."

I stared at the open camper door over his shoulder. I couldn't go back in there. This was my big chance to get to know a movie star, but I couldn't face her again. Not for the lead in the biggest blockbuster of the year. I shook my head and started to turn away. But he still had hold of my elbow.

"Listen, I think it would be nice if you went back. Just for a minute. I'll see that the kid stays out of your way." I hesitated. My heartbeat had subsided to near normal level, and I was able to breathe without gasping. "Come on," he said, "be a good sport." I shrugged my shoulders nonchalantly, which was difficult to do with the knapsack-full-of-bowling-balls still strapped to my back. "Good girl" he said, stepping aside so I could go first.

When I went inside, I tried to keep my eyes averted, but I soon discovered that that wasn't very easy to do. I mean, you can keep your eyes averted from one or two things in a room, but I wanted to avoid the whole room. I couldn't look at Homer, I couldn't look at Gillian Dawn, I couldn't even look at the wardrobe lady. Even the dog, blonde and beautiful Judy, gave me a chill. But when she came over to me as if I were an old friend, I started to play with her. At least it gave me something to do. I could sense the director making gestures over my shoulder, and he and Homer left the camper together.

"Why don't you take a coffee break, Marie?" Miss Dawn said to the plump woman who was fixing a bow on one of the dresses hanging against the wall.

Marie glanced at me and smiled. Then, picking up

a sweater from the chair, she left the camper behind the others.

Gillian Dawn looked up at me. "Come over here. I'd like to talk to you."

I went over slowly, trying to walk straight and tall and proud, like Mary, Queen of Scots, going to the headsman. But all the books strapped to my back made me feel more like the Hunchback of Notre Dame. I sat down where she indicated and let the knapsack slide off my shoulders onto the floor.

"Let's see now, your name was . . ."

"Cynthia. Cynthia Starrett. But they call me Cici."

"Good . . . good . . . I like that. Who's they?"

"Huh?"

"Who calls you Cici? Your family, your friends?"

I nodded.

"How many are in your family?"

"Just my brother and me. And my mother and father."

"Oh. That's too bad. I really would have preferred a bigger family, like the Waltons."

"Well, I have a grandmother. She lives three doors down."

"That's neat," she said emphatically, pointing a scarlet fingernail in my direction. "How old are you, Cici?"

"Thirteen."

"Good. Good! And you live here in Schuyler?"

I nodded again. This sure was a strange conversation. I could almost see her checking off a big list in her mind.

"You go to Schuyler Central?"

"Yes, I do. Miss Dawn, why are you . . ."

"Grade?"

"Eighth."

"Super. Absolutely super. You are *perfect*. A little on the tall side, but otherwise *perfect*."

I stared at her.

"Well, I mean, do you know how long I've been looking for someone like you? And here you just tumble right through that door!"

"You've been looking for someone like me?"

"Yessiree, Cynthia Starrett. You are perfect casting for the part I have in mind!" And she giggled as if she had indeed made a magnificent discovery.

My heart started to pound again. It was happening after all. The fortune-teller was right. And to think that a moment ago I was lying in the gutter, in despair!

"Oh, Miss Dawn, thank you. Thank you! You won't regret this. Oh, and I'm sorry, really I am, for what I said before about Homer. I'm sure he's really a very fine person. It's just that, as you guessed, I'm an actress, like you. And I knew if I just got a chance to see you . . ."

She was pacing up and down, glancing out the door as I spoke. There was an electricity about her, almost as if she were giving off sparks. It's what they mean when they talk about star quality, I guess. I couldn't keep my eyes off her. I couldn't help wondering if she had gotten some of those same sparks from me. If that was why she was giving me my big break . . .

She leaned out the door and called to one of the crew, "Joe, have you seen my kid around?"

"He went off somewhere, Miss Dawn. You want me to round him up?"

"Would you, please? Thanks."

She closed the door and turned back to me.

"It's so incredible how much you and my son have in common. Really remarkable." I must have looked dubious, because she charged on, "You're almost like twins. You're both thirteen, both in the eighth grade, both at Schuyler Central . . ." My mouth fell open so far at that last bit of information I must have looked like a seal at feeding time. "Are you surprised? Yes, it's true! He's enrolled here while I do the movie."

I wasn't exactly thrilled at the news that Homer was going to be in my grade, but with a little luck I could avoid him all term. "But the *part*," I wanted to scream at her, "tell me about the part!"

She took a breather and lit a long, filter-tipped cigarette.

"I know what you're thinking," she said, waving it around cheerfully. "Cancer country! That's what my ex-husband used to call it."

She opened the door and looked out again impatiently. Then she left it ajar and leaned on the edge of the dressing table. She seemed very fidgety. We were silent for a moment. I wanted to ask her, "What does Homer have to do with your giving me a part?" Did she need his approval?

Then suddenly he was standing in the doorway with a container of coffee in his hand. I looked at him with new interest, knowing now who he was, but my second impression was no better than my first. His hair was sand-colored and stood out all around his head as if each strand were a rebel fighting its own private war. And his skin was like chalk, which was surprising when you thought about him living in California.

"Where'd you go off to?" Gillian Dawn demanded, taking the coffee from him and putting it down on the dressing table. "Never mind, guess what!" Here it comes, I thought. She's going to explain about the part, maybe thank him for bringing me right to her door. "Cynthia here is in the eighth grade at Schuyler! She's the same age as you and everything." Why was she going on about us being the same age and being in the same grade? Why didn't she get to the point? She put her arm on my shoulder and pulled me over to where he stood. She smelled wonderful. "Cynthia, or Cici as her friends call her," she said, smiling at me conspiratorially—here it comes, I thought: *is playing the ingenue in my next film*—"is going to be your friend!"

My head snapped around like in that scene in *The Exorcist.* "What?" I cried.

"I told you I had a delicious part for you!"

"A part. You said a part!"

"Yes, well, we're all playing parts, Cici. All the world's a stage and all that. It's just a figure of speech."

"No, it's not!" I heard my voice loud and shrill, the words rushing out of my mouth as if they wanted to get away from me. "You promised. . . . I mean, you two . . . you're both . . ." I stood there, feeling limp and suddenly mute.

Gillian Dawn squeezed my shoulders. "Oh, I am sorry, Cici. I didn't realize you were taking me the wrong way." She bit her lip like she was really, really sorry, which made me feel suddenly a whole lot better.

"That's okay," I said, relishing the role of good sport. "It's really not that important, and I have to be getting home."

"But Cici, what about Homer?"

I looked at him and was reminded suddenly of our dog, Ferguson, when he's been caught in a rainstorm. Homer was dry as a bone, but he looked all wet.

"I . . . I really don't think Homer would want to be friends—"

"Oh, but he does, don't you, kid?"

"I can't think of anything that would be more wonderful than being friends with Cici," he said.

There was so much sarcasm in his voice, I couldn't believe it when Gillian Dawn said, "Is he a charmer, or is he a charmer? Just like his father."

"Shoot . . . Ma, shut up, will ya?"

These two were beginning to fascinate me. She wanted me to have a family like the Waltons, and now he was beginning to *sound* like the Waltons. Except that on the Waltons they never told their mother to shut up.

"Homer, don't talk that way to me," Gillian Dawn said, with the pout that was one of her trademarks. "It's mean." Homer stood there sulking. "Come on, Homer," she entreated, "make nice."

To Homer's credit, he looked as if he were going to puke at this last line.

"Listen, Ma," he said, "let Cici go home. We'll see each other in school." He looked over at me and said, "Won't we?" in a disgustedly sweet voice.

"I guess," I echoed, by this time so totally confused I could have been agreeing to the firebombing of the principal's office.

Gillian Dawn was happy.

"Oh, I'm so glad you two are going to be pals. I knew it would work out. I knew it, I knew it." She flung open the door and called to the director, "Bill, will you see that Henry takes her home? By the time he gets back, I'll be ready to go."

"Oh no, that's all right," I protested. "I can walk, it's not far at all."

"Nonsense. You go with Bill. Ciao!" And she hurried me out the door so I could catch up with the director.

When we got out to the road, a long black limousine was waiting. The chauffeur got out, and as if he wasn't a bit surprised, opened the door for me.

I gave him directions and then settled down into incredibly deep black leather. I had never been in a limousine before. It even smelled special. I watched the streets roll by slowly, and I began to feel a little bit like Gillian Dawn. It would be so wonderful to be a part of this world.

Maybe Homer and I could be friends. The thought wasn't so absurd. When my name was up in lights, the story of how it got there would be peppered with all kinds of amusing anecdotes and eccentric characters. The gods obviously had a delicious sense of humor. First there was Benny Krupchik. Now . . . Homer Montague.

What I had to do was forget the fact that he had played a gross trick on me; forget that he talked through his nose; forget that he looked like a soaking-wet Ferguson. The thing to remember was that he was the son of Gillian Dawn, STAR.

I tried to remember that as the limousine slid up to the curb and I got out in front of my house. But as Ferguson bounded out to greet me, his coat all fluffy and dry, I couldn't help noticing—honest and truly—the dog looked better.

5

"Montague . . . Montague . . . Little Monty and the Moonbeams! That's the one," Grandma announced triumphantly. "He was husband number two."

"How many has she had?" I asked, shredding lettuce into little bits as we talked.

"Let's see now. First one was her agent, fellow with an Italian name. Then Little Monty . . . that lasted only about six months. He was a dope fiend, as I recall. Then there was Grant Forrest, the producer. He was old enough to be her father, but he's the one who really made her a star."

"How can you keep track of it all?"

"Well, you have to when you're in the business," she said. "I mean, it's the most excitin' business in the whole world! And once you're a part of it, even a little part"—and she shrugged her shoulders modestly—"it stays with you. Nothin' ever comes close! Oh Cynthia, I can't tell you how thrilled I am that it went so good for you. It's such a bit of luck—that company comin' here! But I knew it would happen. It's your destiny," she said, tossing the last potato into the pot, "and you know what I say, you can't cheat destiny."

She stood gazing out the window for a moment, drying her hands on a towel, and I could see her drifting away from the sink, the potatoes, and tonight's dinner.

But then she put the potatoes on the stove to boil and went in and picked up yesterday's Schuyler *Gazette* again. She had read the article over and over so many times, I was sure she knew it by heart. I began to set the table. On Thursdays, Grandma always eats with us, and we get the supper started before Mom gets home from work.

"Are you sure they don't need any extras?" she called to me from the living room. It was the fourth time she had asked the question.

"Gram, they say so right in that article. Why would they lie?"

"Oh, you know," she said. "They might not want a lot of amateurs hangin' around. But if they knew my credentials . . . Maybe you should just drop off my portfolio. Do you think it needs a more recent picture?"

"Gram," I said, "maybe you should just let them discover you by accident. You know," I said, having a sudden brainstorm, "they may not want anyone who's too professional."

She thought about that for a moment, pacing back and forth, a bright plaid scarf wrapped around her neck because, as she put it, there was a snap in the air.

"Well, maybe you're right, luv. Now, why don't you just sit down here and tell me again, everything that happened. Don't leave nothin' out."

Mercifully the door opened at that moment, and Mom and Dad walked in. I saw Grandma drop the newspaper onto the chair guiltily.

"Hi you two. What's doin'?" Mom said, putting her bag down and going to hang her coat in the closet. Mom is the only person I know who hangs up her coat as soon as she takes it off. I mean, it doesn't get to rest for a minute. Not on the floor, not on a chair, not anywhere.

"Nothin', nothin' at all, Maureen," Grandma said, winking at me so broadly my mother would have had to be blind not to notice.

"Hi Mom! Hi Dad!"

"Hi there," Dad said, tossing his jacket on a chair and picking up the newspaper. "What's new at the zoo?"

That's what he always asks me about school. Before I had a chance to answer, Walter came bounding down the stairs.

"Dad, can I go to the movies on Saturday with Kenny?"

"Huh?" Dad said, not looking up from the newspaper.

"Can I, Dad? Please . . . can I?"

"You've seen it already."

"No, I haven't. *Death in the Arcade* is playing."

"Oh . . . that's over at the Cinema."

I get so annoyed with Walter sometimes. The Star's not good enough for him anymore. He has no *loyalty*.

"It's too expensive over there," I said.

"Who asked you?"

"Hey, you two, don't start. I've had a tough day and I'm bushed. We'll see, Walter."

"But, Dad . . ."

"We'll see, Walter."

Walter turned and glared at me before he stomped back up the stairs.

"What happend, Walt?" Grandma asked my dad.

"We got another estimate on the roof. Higher than Martin's."

I went into the kitchen where Mom was inspecting dinner. I don't like to be around when Grandma and Dad talk about the Star. Dad's always so gloomy, and Grandma's always trying to cheer him up.

"Whatcha doin', Mom? I fixed the salad."

"I know, dear. I'm just reshredding the lettuce."

I looked over her shoulder. My pieces weren't small enough, I guess. Mom likes to redo things. She's one of those perfectionists. People like that can't help themselves.

"I'll set the table," I said. (I wanted to give her plenty of time to reset it.) When I was finished, I told Mom I wanted to start my homework, so I could go up to my room.

I was almost relieved that Mom and Dad came home when they did. Ever since I returned in the limousine two days ago, Grandma's been in orbit. I told her about my meeting with Gillian Dawn and her son, rewriting the script a little to make my role a little more Nancy Drew and a little less Sylvia Birdbrain. But the more I talked about it, the more Grandma wanted to know. It was as if she couldn't get enough of it. And, of course, next to meeting Gillian Dawn herself, Grandma's greatest ambition now was to meet Homer Montague.

That was something Grandma and I had in common; *I* was dying to see him, too.

Two days had gone by, and I hadn't caught a glimpse of him. I waited for some of the kids to mention that Gillian Dawn's son was in school; it hadn't been mentioned in the paper, but he couldn't come to school forever without someone finding out who he was. But no one said a word.

We were sitting in the cafeteria at lunchtime on Friday, and I was letting my eyes roam over the large noisy room, like a radar scanner. It had gotten to be my regular routine. The entire eighth grade ate at the same time, so he had to be here *someplace.* Unless Henry came and picked him up so he could go to a fancy restaurant to eat. The splendor of his lifestyle was something I couldn't even begin to imagine.

"Wake up! Wake up! Come on, space cadet, come back to us!" Nancy said, snapping her fingers in front of my face.

I pushed her hand away irritably. "Stop it. I was just thinking."

"About what?"

"Uh . . . some homework I didn't do." I finished my sandwich and stood up, pretending to stretch, but really to get a good view of the lunchroom.

And there he was.

He was sitting at the end of a long table by the door. There were some other kids at the table, but they didn't seem to notice he was there. They were talking and fooling around, but none of them even looked in his direction.

I sat back down with all kinds of feelings bouncing around inside of me. I was hoping he'd look over and wave, and then I could wave back. But he never even looked up. He was hunched over the table, reading a book and pushing the food into his mouth halfheart-edly. It must be awful, I thought, not to know any-body in a big school like this. Then I brightened. He did know somebody. He knew me! Suddenly I felt like a missionary, or one of the early suffragettes, set on fire with zeal for the wonderful work I was about to do. I shoved my chair back and elbowed my way across the cafeteria, ignoring Nancy's "Hey, where ya going?" I felt a sense of excitement steal over me. I was the only one in this whole place who was on speaking terms with the son of Gillian Dawn!

"Hi there!" I said when I was close enough to the table so he'd have a chance to hear me. But it obviously wasn't close enough, because he never moved. "HI THERE!" I repeated, almost bellowing it this time. Three other kids at the table looked up, but I didn't know any of them, and they quickly went back to their conversation. Finally he lifted his head and looked around, as if he wanted to make sure I was talking to him. Maybe he wasn't convinced, because he still didn't say anything.

"How've you been?" I persevered.

"Okay," he said, blinking at me.

I have these strange impressions sometimes. Right

then and there I decided that Homer Montague looked like a newborn baby chick . . . if it had been hatched by Woody Allen. Since he was sitting in front of a crumpled-up paper bag, I said, "Finished your lunch?"

"Yeah."

"Wanna meet some kids?"

He seemed to think about that one for a minute. Then slowly he got up and followed me, without saying a word.

I began to have some second thoughts as we retraced our way back to my table. What if he told them about my "visit" to the set?

Nancy was looking at me expectantly as I reached her chair. "Where'd you go?" she asked.

"I want you to meet somebody," I said.

I turned, and he was standing there looking like a whole different person. He had the half smile on his face that I remembered from the first time we met.

I clapped my hands dramatically for quiet. "Hey, you guys, I want you to meet a new kid at Schuyler."

Mark and Benny were at the next table, and they turned and stared at me.

"Gang," I said, really warming to my new role, "This is Hom—"

"Harry. Harry Montague," the voice boomed out beside me, and I swung around to see him glaring at me.

"Harry?" I echoed dumbly.

"That's right," he said, "*Harry*."

The threat was clear: *You tell them my name is Homer, and I'll tell them what a fool you made of yourself the other day.*

45

Gradually the din at the two tables subsided as each kid in turn mumbled "Hi" or "How ya doin'." Mark kicked a chair over and motioned Homer to sit down. He lowered himself into it with the easy assurance of Robert Redford settling down for an interview.

"So where ya from, Harry?" Mark asked. Mark was really the nicest boy in our group, and it was just like him, I thought, to be the first to welcome someone new.

"All over. The coast mainly."

"Your folks get transferred?"

He hesitated a moment. "Not exactly. My mom's here, uh, working."

Wasn't he going to tell them who he was? I was frantic. My tenuous hold on stardom would be snapped if he didn't admit who he was.

"Boy, talk about modesty!" I began.

"Why don't you mind your own business?" he said, so low that none of the others could hear.

"You can't keep it a secret," I hissed.

"Keep what a secret?" Nancy said. "What are you two whispering about?"

"Go ahead, big mouth, why don't you tell them?" he said, like I was about to announce to the whole world that he still slept with a night-light.

My mouth felt dry, but there was no turning back now.

"Hom— Harry's mom is . . . Gillian Dawn," I said.

There was a collective gasp and a lot of mumbling all around us. Jody was the first to speak.

"We should have known," she said, nodding wisely. "He looks just like her."

"Where're you staying?" someone else asked.

"We've rented a house on the river. I think it's called Rocky Cliff."

"You think? Don't you know?" Benny said, laughing.

"Yeah. It's called Rocky Cliff."

I noticed the sea of faces around the table had multiplied as the news of who he was spread out from our little group.

"I guess you know a lot of the stars." It was Jody again, not even trying to conceal her adoration.

A shadow crossed his face. "Some" was all he answered.

Somebody else started to ask a question, but the warning bell rang, and everybody began shoving back chairs and bolting for the doors.

I stood up and had to restrain myself from taking him by the hand, as if he were a two-year-old.

"Tell me where your next class is," I said sweetly, "and I'll help you find it."

"It's calculus, and I can find it myself," he said.

"You're taking calculus?" I asked, not sure I had heard right.

He didn't bother to answer as he headed for the door. I followed him, with Nancy snapping at my heels. We had English next, and we'd probably be late again, but I knew she wouldn't go to class without me. Not today.

"Are you sure you don't need my help?" I called after him anxiously, but he was already down the hall and rounding the corner as we came out. I sure hoped Nancy was impressed with the intimacy of our relationship.

I couldn't tell what she was thinking, because all she

said was "Hey, we'd better run or we'll be late!" And she grabbed my arm and dragged me after her down the stairs.

We got to English just as the bell rang and grabbed two seats in the back. Nancy started scribbling furiously. She passed me a note that read: Wre mt? Hw kno GD? Wht lk?

I stared straight ahead, as if intently drinking in every word that fell from the lips of Miss Scott as she dissected a declarative sentence. She was a middle-aged, plain-looking woman, whose only redeeming quality as far as I was concerned was her genuine love of the theater. She had never married, and I know that's supposed to be liberated, but she was what Grandma called an old maid. She wore a cardigan sweater thrown over her shoulders, no matter what the weather, and her glasses were always attached by a cord that hung around her neck.

I glanced down at the note and, translating the shorthand that we had perfected back in the fourth grade, I read: Where did you meet him? How do you know Gillian Dawn? What's he/she like?

I shook my head imperceptibly, so Nancy would know that I just couldn't answer. Not now.

But by the time we got off the school bus, she had worn me down.

"I went to the set," I admitted finally.

"But how did you get in? I thought no visitors were allowed?"

"Well, no ordinary visitors," I began, "but you know, my grandmother still has some Hollywood connections. The set's open to people in the business."

I felt a little guilty about the lie, but it felt good to see the impressed look on Nancy's face. Even though she'd never admit it, I know that she thinks Grandma is kind of silly with all her talk about Hollywood. So in a way, I told myself, it was a good lie. It was for Grandma.

"So, tell me, what's she really like? Is she gorgeous or is she really an old hag? She couldn't be too old . . . but then again, if she's got a kid our age . . ." Nancy went on, asking questions and answering them herself. "Can you imagine being a movie star's kid? He must know everybody. I bet he comes home from school, and there's Michael Jackson sitting on the porch. Or is it 'patio' out there? I couldn't stand it. I mean it, I'd freak out. Of course, you could get used to it, I guess. . . ."

I waved good-bye to Nancy as we reached my house, and I went up and opened the door in a kind of daze. Walter had gotten home first and was watching a soap opera. My mom would kill him if she knew, but I didn't turn it off. We all need our fantasies.

The world that Nancy was envying, that would be my world someday. I had a wonderful warm feeling from having that secret tucked inside me. I was halfway into that world right now. I looked out the window and watched Nancy go up the street. I had that "apart" feeling again. I wasn't really like Nancy or any of the other kids. There was a wonderful world beyond Schuyler, and there were a few places reserved out there for very special people. I was going to be one of them.

And even though he didn't know it yet, a certain person was going to help me.

6

Even the kids who think Tank Mullaney is a great science teacher admit that he's pretty strange. Take that name. He's listed in the P.T.A. directory as William, but everyone—all the other teachers and even some of the parents—calls him Tank. He used to be a tank commander in the Marines, and I don't think he ever fully recuperated. He talks to us like we're recruits, in this deep, gravelly voice, referring to us by last names only. "Starrett," he'll yell, "let's see what you can do with this here formula I've put on the board." Then he adds, "On the double!" even if you're sitting in the first row and you can almost reach the board by leaning out of your seat. Another favorite bit of dialogue: "Let's get the lead out of those pants!"

Anyway, you can imagine how thrilled I was when he announced one day in the middle of science lab that we were going on a wilderness hike that would "test our mettle." If Mr. Belvedere, the very refined person who heads our art department, told us he was taking us on a hike that would test our mettle, I'd know what to expect. Squishy sneakers. But when Mr. Mullaney said he was going to test our mettle, visions of that snake pit in *Raiders of the Lost Ark* began to dance in my head.

And it's not because, as Nancy claims, I am allergic to sweat.

We had to take a permission slip home to be signed by a parent or guardian. I tried to get my dad to refuse to sign it. I told him I had been in pain ever since I twisted my ankle getting down from the bleachers where I had been sitting out gym class. But he didn't believe me. He thought the nature hike was a great idea. It'll get me away from all those old movies I watch on television, he said. I think I was adopted. He couldn't be my real father.

There were two classes going together, and we were paired off as if we were boarding the ark: boy, girl, boy, girl. Guess who I got? Right. Homer Montague.

I didn't know whether to laugh or cry. If I had gotten some big brawny brute, I would have felt a lot safer. Then again, a big brawny brute might have charged gung ho into the wilderness and led us into all the terrible things I was determined to avoid—like bugs. (I've decided it's not just that bugs are slimy, or crawly, or furry, that I can't stand; what really gets me about them is that they're always in such a hurry. I can't be the only person to have noticed that they're always rushing. What are they up to?)

Thinking it over as we boarded the bus (we were taking the bus to the edge of the jungle swamp that was going to test our mettle), I decided it was better I was paired with a kindred soul. Somebody like me who was more comfortable sitting in a red velvet seat, tenth row center, on opening night.

"Hi," I said. "We're partners."

He let out an inexcusably loud sigh and said "I know" in a voice that sounded like he had just been denied a last-minute stay of execution.

"You feel the same as I do, huh?" I said.

"What?"

He had this habit, I was beginning to notice, this annoying habit of pretending not to understand what I was saying, as if I were speaking a Polynesian dialect never heard by modern man.

"You feel the same as I do about this stupid hike," I said. "You look like you're going to the gallows," I added, in case he still didn't understand me.

We shoved our knapsacks up onto the rack and slid into our seats just in time to avoid being trampled by the next wave of kids boarding the bus.

"I don't mind *hikes*," he said.

End of quote.

I sat there glaring at him for a minute. What was that supposed to mean? I knew what that was supposed to mean. He just didn't like being my partner.

I turned to the window and studied the trees, the pavement, the cars, anything, as we pulled out of the school parking lot and headed God-knows-where. If he wasn't a kindred soul, what was I going to do? He was no Harrison Ford, that was for sure. If we got trapped in a cave full of snakes, and I was screaming for help, he'd just look at me blankly and say, "What?"

Nancy had gotten Joey Steinberg for a partner. Joey was the funniest boy in our grade—also the smallest. She, too, was unprotected, but at least she'd die laughing.

In a way it would be kind of neat if something really gruesome happened to me on this trip. That would teach Tank to test the mettle of someone who didn't want her mettle tested. And it would teach my dad, too. He'd realize it was a lot better to have a daughter safe at home watching old movies in one piece than to have her splattered all over the bottom of a cliff. Or maybe lost forever in a cave somewhere.

It has been fourteen years since the lovely young Cynthia Starrett disappeared inside this cave while on a wilderness hike with her eighth-grade classmates. But not a day goes by that someone doesn't come to lay roses at the entrance of the cave. Did she ever escape? Is she perhaps even now wandering aimlessly down some strange street in some strange town, having lost her memory? (Scene shifts to a strange street in a strange town.) Cynthia Star, looking wan and haggard (but still incredibly beautiful, with every hair still in place after fourteen years), wanders aimlessly. A young detective (played by—Harrison Ford was too old. I was getting a little bored with Timothy Hutton—Matt Dillon!) turns and stares after her. A flicker of recognition darts across his face. He rushes up behind her and says—

"Are you aware that you're talking to yourself?"

"Wha . . ." I jumped in my seat and turned to face Homer, sitting there like a gnome on the seat of judgment. "I was not."

"Of course you were. You're always wandering

around like a refugee from *Lost in Space*. Hey, that's pretty good!" He whipped out a notebook and wrote furiously for a moment. Then he snapped the notebook shut and stuffed it back into his jacket pocket.

"What did you just write down?"

"Nothing."

"How could you write nothing? I saw you write something. Was it something about me?"

He stared at me. "Of course not. Why would I write something about you?"

"Well, you were talking to me and then you went like 'Hurrah!' and wrote something down. So what was it, a laundry list?"

"Not that it is any of your business, but I am a writer. And writers always carry notebooks and jot things down."

"Oh, you want to be a writer when you grow up!"

Again the stare, as if he couldn't believe anyone as stupid as me was allowed to walk the streets without a leash.

"No, not when I 'grow up.' Why should I wait till then? I am a writer now. You, of course, wouldn't understand."

"Oh no? Then tell me, Norman Mailer, what have you written?"

"Three plays and one short novel. The novel hasn't been published yet, but a New York publisher is interested. The plays have all been performed in little theatre groups out on the coast. Why? Do you want my autograph?"

"No, thank you" was all I could think of to say.

Among other things, Homer Montague had the nasty habit of always getting the last word.

We arrived at the wilderness camp a little after nine, and I watched anxiously as the buses roared off down the road, not to be seen again until six o'clock tonight. If buses could laugh, that's what they were doing, guffawing as they tore off down the road to civilization.

We started on the trail after enduring a thirty-minute lecture by Tank, who kept reminding us to watch out for our "buddies." If this trip was perfectly safe, how come we had to keep watching out for one another?

Nancy and Joey came with our group as we started into the woods. I told myself this wasn't too bad. I tried to concentrate on the beauty of nature. If I were a poet, and I wanted to lie, I would tell you how the sun was dappling through the leaves, filtering happiness all over the place. But the weather was the pits. It wasn't raining yet, but the weatherman had said, "chance of showers." I was sure Tank was secretly praying for a monsoon.

"Did you notice," Nancy was saying to me, "how Mullaney is always referring to us as men? 'It's okay, men, follow me' and 'Good work, men.' He even said this hike was going to separate the men from the boys."

We had started up what looked like one of the Himalayas, and I was puffing so badly I could barely grunt an answer. Nancy is very sensitive to sex discrimination, and while I might have been truly indignant under different circumstances, sex discrimination was, at the moment, the *least* of Tank Mullaney's transgressions. I seriously suspected he was deranged and had brought us all out here to die of exposure.

Nancy and Joey began to pull farther and farther ahead of us. Everybody seemed to be pulling farther and farther ahead of us. But Homer stayed within yelling distance. I began to feel like a dog he had brought along, let off the leash as long as I stayed nearby.

I began to think about what he had said. It was true, why wait till you grow up to be what you want to be? I'm an actress, why shouldn't Homer be a writer? Maybe he was a boy wonder. That would account for his strange moods. Maybe he was a genius. I'd have to be more understanding. If I didn't understand the artistic temperament, who did?

I never saw the branch. Obviously I never saw it. If I had seen it—a long, sharp, prickly stick lying across my path—would I have tucked my foot neatly under it and flipped over into space? The pain was excruciating, and I literally had stars in my eyes for a moment. After a few minutes, there was a babble of voices above me, and I tried to turn my head and look up.

"Don't move, Starrett. Better check out that ankle."

About a dozen hands helped me into a sitting position, and I sat there, in a daze, while Tank Mullaney gingerly probed my ankle. It throbbed.

"Nothing's broken," he barked. "Think you can keep up with the rest of us?" It was like having a conversation with a Doberman pinscher.

I remembered all those old war movies where they think the guy is going to slow them down, so they leave him behind to die.

"I'll walk," I promised feebly. But when they helped me to my feet, the pain shot through my ankle like a bullet.

"I'm sure it's not broken. It's just a sprain, Starrett."

"But it hurts!" I said, feeling a lump in my throat. If I started to cry in front of everyone, like a little kid in a playground, I'd have to throw myself off a cliff.

"Hmm. Don't like to have a casualty. Never had one before," he said testily.

"You never had Cici along before," someone said, and there was a wave of laughter through the group.

"I'll radio the bus to come back for you."

"No . . . no. Don't do that," I said. I wouldn't give them the satisfaction.

"Well, I don't want you falling behind when we get to the hilly terrain," he said.

When we get to the hilly terrain . . . Where were we now?

"I'll stay with her," a voice behind me said wearily.

I didn't turn around. I knew who it was.

"Tell you what. You two break for lunch here. When we swing back this afternoon, we can pick you up for the last leg of the hike."

And with that, he marched off looking like John Wayne in *The Sands of Iwo Jima*. A pot-bellied John Wayne.

I stood there, putting all the pressure on my left foot and holding my right foot off the ground like a stork.

"You want to sit down?" Homer asked.

I nodded, and he helped me settle onto a nearby rock.

"I'm really sorry you have to miss out on the, er, fun," I said.

He screwed up his face like, once again, I had said something dumb. "I'm not missing anything."

"I thought you enjoyed hikes."

"I never said that."

"You did too!"

"No, I didn't."

"You said . . ."

"I don't mind hikes. That was what I said. I always know what I've said."

Oh God, I thought, he was such a prune. I tried to get my fantasy machine going, but just being near him seemed to jam it up.

"It's only a sprain," he said. "You'll be fine in a day or two."

I nodded. We sat in silence for a moment. "Are you hungry?" I asked.

"Yeah," he said, looking surprised, like it hadn't occurred to him before. "Might as well eat."

We got our sandwiches out of our knapsacks and opened our sodas.

"What did you mean when you said that I wouldn't understand?" I asked him.

"What?" There was that look again.

"Back on the bus. You said you were a writer *now*, and I wouldn't understand."

"Oh, yeah. Right."

"What did you mean?" I repeated.

He ate his sandwich for a minute, taking two or three bites before he answered me.

"Because you're always thinking about what you're

going to be, or what you're going to do. You don't do anything *now*."

"That's not true!" I said, as indignantly as if he had just called me an ax murderess.

"Sure it is. I listen. That's what writers do, you know, listen. I've heard kids talking about you. You didn't want to be a cheerleader, you wouldn't help decorate for the square dance next week. . . ."

"You don't listen, you eavesdrop."

"You call it eavesdrop, I call it listening."

"My *friends*," I said, putting enough emphasis on the word so he would understand he was not a member of that elite group, "allow me to be myself. I am not like they are, and they understand that. They may tease me a little, but they understand."

"Understand what? That you think you're better than they are?"

"I didn't say that!"

"That's what it sounded like."

"Well, that's not what it is at all! I just don't . . . have any interest in those sorts of things. I have a specific goal in mind. I'm goal-oriented." (I had read that phrase somewhere, and it had such a nice sound to it that I decided then and there that's what I was.) "I've known almost all my life what I wanted to be, what I *am*."

"And what's that?"

"An actress."

"Egads, you *are* nuts."

"Look, let's not talk about it anymore, okay?"

"Why do you want to be an actress?"

"I don't want to talk about it."

"Come on. I told you I was a writer."

"Because," I answered lamely. "It's . . . it's exciting. You can do anything you want. People admire you, and write you fan letters, and take your picture. You're *famous!*"

"Not all actresses are famous."

"Well, I'm going to be one of the famous ones," I said firmly.

"You don't want to be an actress," he said, with a note of dismissal in his voice. "You want to be a celebrity."

I took a drink of my Coke as if I weren't listening. He had hit a target I'm sure he didn't know he was aiming at.

"Obviously you don't know my background. Movies are in my blood. We own the Star, you see." He stared at me blankly. "The big old movie theatre on Peartree Avenue?"

"Oh."

"So it was kind of preordained that I would be an actress. You can see that, can't you?"

"Nope," he said, in that infuriatingly smug tone of voice, as if he was right and the rest of the world was wrong. "It is not," he said, putting the remains of his lunch back in his bag and getting up to stretch, "the most *worthy* goal I've ever heard of."

"Well, pardon me, Mr. Hemingway."

He moved away without answering and sat on a little knoll where he would have a view of the class coming back.

"Your mother's famous," I said, after we had sat in silence for a while.

"That's right," he said, looking over at me. "And you two are a lot alike. She thinks she's pretty special, too."

"Well, she should! I mean, she *is!* My gosh, aren't you proud of her?"

He didn't answer me.

"Do you know how many kids would die to be in your shoes, to live like you do?"

He still didn't answer me, but I could see his jaw moving like he was chewing something. Or grinding his teeth maybe. He sure was a strange person.

We didn't talk anymore, and the afternoon drifted away slowly. Finally we heard the sound of footsteps and kids laughing in the distance. After sharing an afternoon with the great stoneface, Tank Mullaney would seem like Richard Gere.

"How's the ankle, Starrett?" he barked.

"Fine, sir, just fine," I said, struggling to my feet and standing at attention.

"Knew there was nothing wrong with it! Waste of a good man," he said, gesturing in Homer's direction.

I wanted to protest. I wanted to say, "Sir, are you accusing me of malingering?" But I knew enough to quit when I was ahead. I limped slowly behind Nancy and Joey all the way back to the parking lot.

It was just getting dark as we boarded the bus.

"It was fun," Nancy said, as we took our seats. "Rough, but fun. It's a shame you had to miss it."

"Yeah," Joey added, "it's good to have a little torture now and then."

They should know, if torture was the afternoon's main attraction, I didn't miss a thing.

7

Friday night, Nancy, Jan, Jody, and I got to the square dance just as the caller was setting up. It was the same caller we always had, and I didn't like him. He yelled at us too much.

We grabbed a space on the gym floor, and pretty soon Mark, Benny, Kevin, and Bud joined us. Mark took his place beside me the way he always did at these dances, ever since the fifth grade.

The caller began with his customary list of instructions and don'ts: Don't move until he told you to; don't change sets between numbers; don't make too much noise, or we wouldn't be able to hear his calls.

"He's such a grouch. Why do we use him?" Jody asked.

"My mom said they tried to get someone else this year, but he was the only one available," Nancy said.

We started the first reel, and pretty soon everybody was laughing and hooting out loud. We bumped into each other more than we connected. When it was over, the caller announced that there were three late-comers standing by the door, and as others arrived, they could form another set. For the first time, I looked around the gym for Homer, but he wasn't there.

As we started another set, I thought how stupid and unfair he was, saying I didn't like to do things. I liked doing this. I liked whirling around, feeling my long hair floating around my head, getting breathless and dizzy and laughing too much.

The second set ended, and as we tried to catch our breath, the caller said, "One, two, three, four, five, yes, there's eight of you now. Form a set over in that corner," he ordered, and I saw a group of kids move away from the entrance toward the corner of the gym.

This time it was a quadrille, and we really got confused. We tried to listen to the instructions he was calling out, but something was going on in the corner of the gym. We began to strain our necks to see what was happening, but the whirling dancers blocked our view. I was in the middle of switching from Mark to Kevin, arms linked, when the music stopped abruptly.

I looked up at the caller, who stood with his arms folded, his face crimson. Slowly quiet settled over the gym as the kids tried to figure out what had happened. Then suddenly we knew.

The caller's voice boomed out, ignoring the microphone.

"Is the gentleman in the red shirt ready to take his place as the partner of the lady in the yellow sweater?"

"No, he is not!" a younger voice shot back.

Some kids began to giggle, and everyone turned

around to see who the wise guy was. Everyone but me, that is. I knew who it was. I'd know that nasal voice anywhere.

"Young man, there are seven people here who would like to participate in this activity. They cannot unless you join them." Silence. "If you didn't wish to dance, why did you come?" There was an iciness to the caller's slow, deliberate speech that let us know his patience was wearing thin.

"I am here," Homer answered, sounding like the president delivering his State of the Union address, "as an observer."

Oh God, I thought, he's probably got his notebook with him, too.

"Oh," the caller replied sarcastically, "and what have you observed?"

"A lot of very clumsy adolescents, thinking they are graceful, and thereby making a spectacle of themselves."

There was a collective gasp. He was such a jerk! What was he trying to prove? It was one thing to be a loner, which a lot of the kids already decided he was, but he was going to end up being hated.

"Young man, you have thirty seconds to join the group now being formed. After that, you may leave."

You could have heard a pin drop. "Twenty seconds," the caller said. I strained my neck to get a look at Homer. He was trying to look like Mr. Cool, but I could have sworn, even from the distance, that there was perspiration all over his face. "You may leave now, young man," the caller announced. "If you don't, the square dance is over for everyone."

There was a murmur of disgust and protest from the

crowd. Suddenly Homer bolted from his place by the wall and fled out the door.

Some of the kids started to laugh, but a lot of them looked uncomfortable. I saw the chaperones conferring with each other, and then Nancy's mother went up and spoke to the caller. We stood there awkwardly for a few minutes while the caller talked with the chaperones. It looked almost as if they were arguing. Finally he started the music again and began to explain a new set as if nothing had happened. But before we could start, Nancy's mom came over and touched my elbow.

"Cici, would you come with me?"

"Where are you going?" Nancy asked.

"We have to find Harry Montague," her mother said. "We're responsible for him."

"I'll go with you," Nancy said.

"Nancy, Cici is the only one who seems to be Harry's"—she hesitated—"friend." Suddenly it was a stigma. I felt as if I had a deadful disease. "But you can come, too," she said as an afterthought.

"Where'll we look?" I asked Mrs. Irving, as I struggled into my jacket and followed her out to the parking lot.

"Well, let's hope he's just hanging around the school. If he's not, we'll have to go to his house and tell his mother what's happened. That caller had no right to throw him out like that. We're responsible for you kids at something like this."

We drove around the school and the few blocks surrounding it, but there was no sign of "Harry."

"Do you know where they live?" Nancy asked her

mother. It may have been my imagination, but I thought I sensed a note of excitement in her voice.

Mrs. Irving let out a sigh of exasperation. "No, of course not. But the office must have the address," she said, pulling up to the school again. "Come on." And the three of us hurried back inside.

We drove without speaking the four or five miles to the section of Schuyler that bordered the river.

The houses were invisible over here, people said, unless you saw them from a boat. Every once in a while a new one went up, more opulent and extravagant than anything that had been built before. Rocky Cliff was perfectly named. It was a large contemporary home set into the granite side of the cliff. You had to travel up a steep, narrow driveway to get there, and as Mrs. Irving laboriously negotiated turn after turn, I wondered what would happen if somebody were coming the other way. It had to happen, sometime, and when it did, did the person going up have to back down, or did the person going down have to back up?

"What are we going to say? What if he's not here? He couldn't have walked this far," I said.

"We have to let his mother know what happened," Mrs. Irving said nervously.

We pulled into the circular driveway, and I thought I'd never seen so much glass in my life. It was literally a glass house, with just enough wood here and there to keep it from shattering into a million crystals the first time somebody slammed a door.

Mrs. Irving hopped out, hurried up to the huge panelled doors, and rang the bell, with the two of us right behind her. In a moment the door opened, and Henry was standing there.

"Yes?" he said. He was wearing the same black suit as before. Or maybe he had a whole wardrobe of black suits—all the same.

"I'm Barbara Irving, from the school. Have you heard from Harry? He was at the square dance tonight, but he left. Has he been in touch with you?" She paused for a moment, then, as if she was afraid he didn't understand the situation, she said, "Maybe I should speak to his mother."

I thought I caught a flicker of surprise cross his face when Mrs. Irving referred to "Harry," but other than that, his face was like a marble statue's. "One moment, please," he said, as he soundlessly closed the door in our faces.

He was back immediately. "Ms. Dawn isn't able to see you right now, but she wishes me to inform you that her son is quite safe."

"Where is he? Is he here?"

"Yes, he's at home. He rang us up from town, and I went and got him."

I could hear Mrs. Irving let out a sigh of relief. "I'm so glad he's all right. You see, we never let children leave a school function . . ."

"That's quite all right. I'm sure Ms. Dawn doesn't hold you responsible." He turned and looked straight at me. "You're Cynthia Starrett?"

I looked around for a moment, as if there might be another Cynthia Starrett in the crowd. Then I nodded my head, and he stepped back a bit, opening the door wider.

"Ms. Dawn would like to speak with you." Then to Mrs. Irving, "We'll see that Cynthia gets home safely."

Nancy looked like she was going to explode with curiosity, but her mother only looked confused.

"Well, I guess it's all right. Cici?"

"I'll be fine, Mrs. Irving, you go on home. See you tomorrow, Nance," I said, trying to sound casual.

I stepped inside, Henry closed the door noiselessly behind me, and . . . remember that scene in *The Wizard of Oz*, when Dorothy first lands there and she says to Toto, "I have a feeling we're not in Kansas anymore"?

Well, I know just how she felt.

8

Once inside, my gaze went straight up. It had nowhere else to go. The house was three stories high, but there was nothing but air between the ground floor and the roof. When I looked up, all I saw was a skylight and an open stairwell. There must have been rooms up there somewhere, but I couldn't see them from where I was standing. There was a lot of rock, and plants and flowers were growing everywhere. It was almost like a jungle. And in the middle of the entryway, like a giant centerpiece, a waterfall was splashing peacefully.

A voice pierced the stillness.

"Henry, what's taking you so long? Where is she?"

Henry nodded for me to follow him across a polished stone floor and down two steps into a large glass-walled living room. Here, too, there was the feeling of being in the wilderness. Through the glass,

I could see lush tropical plants bathed in light, and the silhouette of gnarled trees etched against the night sky.

Gillian Dawn met us halfway into the room. She had a drink in one hand, and with the other she motioned Henry out of the room.

"Come on," she said brusquely, "we have to talk."

She was wearing a long red caftan, trimmed in gold, and there was a heavy perfume in the air. As she folded herself onto a cushion in front of the fire blazing in the big, stone fireplace, she gestured for me to join her.

I went over and carefully lowered myself onto a cushion facing her. The fire burning in the fireplace gave off the only light in the room besides the lights outside in the garden.

It had finally happened. What was really going on, at this very moment, was better than any fantasy I could conjure up. Even *my* imagination couldn't improve upon this: the exotic house, the brightly colored gown, the blazing fire, the smell (Incense! That's what it was. They used it in a little curio shop in town). Even without the incense, the whole house had a certain smell to it. Maybe this was what having lots of money smelled like. But I knew it was more than that. It was a mixture of fine things, like flowers brought in from the garden (huge bunches of them), and all the furniture being so new that it didn't have any stains on it, and crystal and silver things shining all around the room. I decided they must be contributing to the smell, too.

"First of all," Gillian Dawn began, and I snapped

back to attention (but it was so bizarre—reality was the fantasy here!), "I want you to know I really don't blame you for what happened tonight. You just weren't prepared." What was she saying? I started to speak, but she plowed on. "So," she said, blowing mock kisses all around the room, "forgive, forgive! We won't be mad at . . . Cici? That was it, wasn't it? That's what your family calls you?" The way she said *family* she made it sound like a rare species of bird.

I nodded. I'm not sure I could have spoken if I tried. It was as if she were acting out one of her roles, and I was her audience of one. How wonderful it must be to be so magnificent all the time. She leaned over and whispered conspiratorially.

"This won't change anything, will it? I mean, you're still going to be the kid's friend, aren't you?" Again I nodded. She seemed pleased and started to sit back, but then, as if caught by surprise, she peered at me closer and said, "Good God, are those your real eyelashes?"

"Of course they are, Miss Dawn."

"Please call me Gillie, everyone does. Dawn is just a press agent's idea. My real name, the one I had when I was your age, was Gilden Dermer." She threw her head back and laughed that familiar throaty laugh. "Isn't this cozy?" she said. "I wish you were my daughter. You have such possibilities. I could teach you all about makeup and clothes. I would love to have had a daughter. I wanted Homer to be a girl, but you know how he is, he'll never do anything you want him to."

Gillian Dawn wanted me to be her daughter. My

mind reeled at the idea. "I would love to be your daughter!" I blurted out. Then I realized how awful that must sound. "I mean, we have a lot in common. My grandmother's a lot like you. Her stage name was Polly Mason. Maybe you're heard of her?"

She looked a little vague and then shook her head. Maybe I shouldn't have spoken. People as glorious as Gillian Dawn aren't used to a dialogue. They're always the star. But she was silent, as if she wanted to hear more, so I went on.

"My grandmother made three movies: *Roaring Twenties*, *Dark Victory*, and *No Time for Comedy*. She was only an extra, but you can see her clear as day. *Roaring Twenties* was on 'The Late Show' once, and I got to stay up and watch it. There was a scene in a nightclub, with all these people whooping it up, and you can see Grandma clear as day, right over James Cagney's shoulder. He was the star of the picture, you know. She even talked to him once. He bumped into her on the set, and he said 'Excuse me' nice as anything. She says he was just like a regular person."

I had almost run out of breath, I was talking so fast, but I didn't seem to be able to stop. "We're still in the business," I said. "We own the Star, you know. The movie house over on Peartree Avenue? My grandparents bought it over forty years ago, when they came here from Hollywood. Gee, my grandmother is thrilled that you're here!"

"Is she?"

"Oh yes. She'd die if she knew I was here, right in your house, talking to you like you were a real person!"

"That's very nice. Maybe you can bring Granny around to the set sometime."

"You mean it, Miss Dawn? Uh . . . Gillie," I corrected myself.

"Of course I do," she said, in a tone of voice that made me know, somehow, that the subject was closed. Then she began peering at me again. "You've got incredible bones, you know. I'm sure you don't appreciate that yet, but you will."

"Thank you," I said, and then we sat in silence for a moment. I knew I should get up to leave, but I didn't want to. I felt that something needed to be said about tonight, and the square dance, and Homer. "Gillie," I began, my voice barely able to get the name out, "about tonight—"

"What about tonight?"

I spun around at the sound of his voice. Homer was slumped on a couch in a corner of the room. He was almost invisible in the shadows.

"I didn't know you were here," I said.

"Why shouldn't I be? I live here, remember? What are *you* doing here?"

I stood up. "We came over," I said icily, "Nancy and her mother and me, because of the way you acted at the dance." Good. Get him into trouble. I waited for Gillian Dawn to ask me about tonight. But it was Homer who spoke.

"Are you sure? Are you sure you didn't just crawl over to get her autograph?"

"Oh, come on kids, let's just forget the whole thing. Don't worry, she's still going to be your friend, aren't you?" she said, and I realized then that she really didn't want to know anything about what had happened. She was like a beautiful bird that someone was forcing down to earth, its wings flapping in frustration.

Gillian Dawn got up, and as if I didn't exist, floated out of the room, saying to Homer as she reached the door, "Tell Henry to take your friend home."

We stood awkwardly for a moment, then he said, "I'll get Henry," and he started for the door.

"Why'd you do that tonight?" I demanded.

"You noticed, huh?"

"Noticed? The whole eighth grade noticed. You caused some scene."

"Did I? Good."

"Why? Why good? That's so babyish."

He glared at me. "I don't have to account to you for my behavior. I don't have to account to anyone!" Then he left, and I heard him calling out to Henry that I was ready to go.

I got to ride in the limousine again. I looked at my watch as we passed under a streetlight. 10:10. I'd get home before Mom would have a chance to start worrying. The limousine pulled up and stopped, and I jumped out without waiting for Henry to open the door.

"Good night," I called and started up the walk. I saw the drapes in the living room window move, and I knew somebody had been watching me.

Mom was in the kitchen doorway.

"Mrs. Irving called just now to see if you were home yet. She told me what happened."

I tried to keep my voice casual, which was hard to do since my mind was bouncing around with all the images of the evening.

"It was no big deal. You know Nancy's mom. She gets hyper. Where's Dad?" I asked. I wasn't really that curious, but I wanted to get my mother's eyes off me. I felt like she knew I had actually said "I would love to be your daughter!" to somebody else.

"Down at the Star. Where else? The burner broke down again. They're going to have to do something soon," she said with a sigh. "We can't go on pouring good money after bad."

"What we should do is remodel it. We'd make a fortune."

"Oh Cici, honey, you don't understand."

"I do too! Dad only cares about the money part of it, so I'm being very practical. Grandma's never gonna sell the Star, no matter how much Dad would like it, so my suggestion makes sense."

"Cici . . . what's come over you? He doesn't just care about the money, although it *is* one consideration." She went back into the kitchen but returned almost immediately and stood in the doorway with a worried expression on her face. "Cici, it may be time that your father got a chance to do what *he'd* like to do. Okay? I know you wouldn't want to deny him that, would you?"

It was very quiet all of a sudden. "No. Of course not," I said. What was my mother talking about? Whatever it was, it made me uneasy, and it was ruining the euphoric feeling I had brought home with me. "I'd better get to bed," I said. "It's late."

I think my mother was disappointed I didn't want

to talk about it more. But she just said, "Okay, hon, g'night," and went back in and started waxing the refrigerator.

Things were sure getting complicated. I had never thought about my father not being happy managing the Star, really and truly wanting to do something else. It would be like me having to work in an ordinary place like Crandall's all my life, and never ever being famous.

But what else could he do?

Maybe Dad was just trying to be nice and help out by taking over the Star when Grandpa died. Ten years. That was a long time to be doing something you hated.

9

"What was she wearing?" Jody wanted to know.

"Let me tell," Nancy begged. "A red dress. You know, what do they call them . . ."

"A caftan," I volunteered.

"Right. A caftan. Red, with gold threads all through it."

"Wow," Jody said. "I hope I look like that when I get old."

I looked at Nancy and she looked at me, and we both started to giggle at the same time.

"Stop it, you guys! You know what I mean!"

Nancy was taking an absolutely morbid interest in every detail of my visit to Rocky Cliff. She was enjoying it as much as if she had actually been inside the house herself. Grandma says it's called getting a vicarious thrill out of something, like when she reads movie magazines.

We were sitting on the stone steps of the school at

lunchtime and didn't even notice Homer Montague until he loomed over us, mumbling "Excuse me" as he stepped around us, a book in his hand. The three of us silently watched as he walked over to the side of the hill facing the river.

"Where's he going?" Jody asked.

"He sits over there by himself every lunch hour," Nancy said. "I guess he thinks he's too good for us."

"Well, I guess coming from Hollywood, we must all seem pretty boring," Jody said sympathetically.

I didn't say anything. I was wondering if he had overheard our conversation.

It was a couple of days later that I ran into Homer in the media center. He had study period the same time as I did on Wednesdays, so sometimes I saw him in there, but I usually sat with Nancy or Jan. Today I was alone and all the tables were filled, except the one way over in the corner where Homer the hermit had his head buried in a book.

I hesitated for a moment, and then I went over and pulled out the chair. He looked up briefly as my books fell to the table with a thud, then he went back to his reading. I *hate* rude people.

"Hi," I said.

"Hi."

I opened my science notebook and began to study. After a few minutes, I was aware that somebody's eyes were on me. Well, not exactly on me. On my science notes. I looked up, and Homer was trying to read my notes upside down.

"What are you doing?"

"What does it look like I'm doing?"

"It looks like you're trying to read my notes upside down."

"Right."

"Don't you have your own?"

"Nope. Can I borrow yours?"

"I have a test tomorrow. I need them."

"I have the same test. That's why I need to copy somebody's notes."

"Well . . . you can copy mine. But when would you have the chance?"

"How about after school? It won't take long."

I shook my head. "I have to go home right after school."

"So I'll go home with you."

"Well, I . . . I guess that'd be all right. It's the number 3 bus."

"Fine," he said, and we both went back to our notebooks.

But I couldn't concentrate. While I had every intention of crashing into Homer's world, it never occurred to me that he'd visit mine. It would be like bringing E.T. home.

I could feel him still staring, and I looked up.

"Now what's the matter?"

"Sorry. It's just that you remind me of someone."

"Who?"

"My sister."

"Your sister? I thought you didn't have a sister!"

"Well, she wasn't really my sister. We just used to pretend. She was a girl my mom let live with us for a while a few years back. Her name was Rory."

"Was?"

"Yeah. She's dead now."

"Oh gee," I said, "I'm sorry. What happened to her?"

"I don't like to talk about it," he said, shaking his head.

"Oh, I'm sorry," I said again.

But then he went on, "It was a fire. I got out, and Mom got out. But we couldn't get to Rory. She was screaming and screaming. . . ."

"Oh my gosh, Homer, how awful for you and your poor mother," I said, trembling. No wonder he was strange, withdrawn from people. This boy had *suffered*. Gingerly I reached out and touched his hand. "How old was she?"

"My mother?"

"No, no, Rory."

"Who?"

"Rory. The girl who was like your *sister*," I whispered.

"I don't have a sister. Boy, Cici, you of all people should know that!" His face had that smirk I was beginning to recognize and loathe.

"You . . . you made that whole thing up! Why? Why would you make up a horrible story like that?"

Mrs. Fuller rapped a ruler on her desk. That was the signal to lower your voice or get out.

"Took your nose out of the notebook, didn't it?"

I jumped up, grapped my books, and slammed the chair under the table. Again the *rap-rap* of Mrs. Fuller's ruler.

"You are a nut!" I whispered, and I tore out of the center.

I couldn't believe it when I boarded the bus that afternoon and there he was, looking absolutely angelic. I took a seat as far away from him as possible and talked all the way home to Martha Dillon, a sixth grader who lives in my neighborhood.

When we got to my stop, I could see him get up and follow me, but I just ignored him. I continued to ignore him until we were a half block away from my house. Finally I couldn't stand it any longer. Whirling around I screamed, "Why are you such a creep?" I would like to have phrased it better, but he was the writer, not me. To my surprise, he didn't come back with a smart answer.

"I dunno" was all he said.

I just stared at him for a moment, with my mouth hanging open like a Venus's-flytrap. Then we turned in and went up the walk. The door opened just as we were walking up the front steps. Walter came darting out with a Twinkie in one hand and his jacket in the other.

"Hey, put the jacket on, it's getting cold," I said.

"I will," he said over his shoulder as he brushed past us on the front porch. He almost knocked Homer back down the stairs. Since it was my job to keep tabs on Walter after school, I called after him, "Where are you going?"

"Grandma's in there," he yelled back. "She knows."

We went through the front door, and I unloaded my books on the chair in the hall.

"Come on," I said, leading the way into the kitchen.

Grandma was pouring herself a cup of tea. She looked up when she heard us, and a big smile spread over her face.

"Well, well, well, well, you don't have to tell me who your friend is, Cynthia. I'd recognize those dark eyes anywhere. You're Homer Montague, right?"

He shot me a look, but then quickly held out his hand. "That's right, and you're Cici's grandmother, the lady who used to be in movies!"

I didn't think it was possible for someone Grandma's age to blush, but she did.

"Why, Cynthia, you've been borin' this young man. I tell Cynthia all the time, 'Don't go braggin' about me.' People don't care about them times. That's ancient history!" And she gave a soft little giggle. Right before my eyes my grandmother was turning into a teenager and flirting with a thirteen-year-old.

"Uh, Gram, Homer wants to copy some of my notes."

"Well, you go right ahead. I'll fix you some milk and some brownies."

"That's okay, Gram, I'll get . . ."

"That would be real swell of you," he said. "If you're sure it's not too much trouble."

"Of course it wouldn't be no trouble," she said, fluttering around the kitchen.

While Grandma was fixing the snack, I watched Homer. He didn't think I noticed, but he was looking around at everything like he had never been in an ordinary home before. Gram put a plate of brownies and two glasses of milk on the kitchen table. When she left us alone, I took out my notes and tossed them on the table. He had already started eating the brownies. He was still looking around at everything, so I said, "It's not much like your place, is it?"

"Which place is that?"

"Where you live. With the rocks and the fountain and everything."

"No, it's not."

"Well, we think it's perfectly fine!" I said.

"Of course it is. It's charming. Did I say anything?"

"No, but I could tell by the way you were looking around."

"Why are you so crazy?"

"Me? Crazy? Me—crazy? Oh no, Mr. Montague, you can't pull that on me. You're the crazy one, not me!" I was aiming for Katherine Hepburn, but I think it came out sounding more like Walter having one of his fits.

"I'm not the one who lives in dream city," he countered.

"Oh no? What about that story you made up today in the media center? What about the way you sit off by yourself all the time ignoring everyone? What about the square dance? Anyway," I finished lamely, "I think you should behave yourself for your mother's sake. You know, she really worries about you. That's why she asked me to be your friend."

"Don't worry about her. She's not really my mother."

"What?"

"She only pretends to be my mother, because nowadays it's good publicity."

"Homer, that's a terrible thing to say!"

"No kidding. Didn't you know that motherhood is coming back? All these old dames are running around having babies before their biological clocks run out. Isn't that a hoot? I read all about it in a magazine."

The conversation was beginning to make me very uncomfortable. "So what does that have to do with your mother? She must have been pretty young when you were born."

"Sure she was. Twenty-one. She didn't marry my dad until two months before I was born."

I could feel my face getting red. "She *told* you that?"

"She didn't have to. I can count, you know. Anyway, she didn't even look at me until a year ago."

I sat down uneasily in the chair opposite him and took a brownie. He was wearing me down again. Even if almost everything Homer says turns out to be a lie, while he's saying it, it sounds so true. And like it must have hurt so much.

"I stayed with my grandmother when I was little," he went on, "then when she got sick, I started going to boarding school. The only reason I'm here now is because my shrink told her to bring me along."

"Your shrink . . . you go to a psychiatrist?"

"Sure," he said, helping himself to the last brownie. "Don't you?"

I burst out laughing, then stopped. "Homer, I've never even met anyone who actually went to a psychiatrist. But, of course, movie stars always go to one, don't they? I never realized their kids did, too."

"Only the interesting ones," he said, getting that look in his eyes again.

I opened my science notebook slowly and shoved it in front of him. "I don't believe a word of what you say, Homer Montague."

"Not a word? How about a syllable? That part about her getting married two months before I was born, you can check on that. They don't hide that kind of thing like they used to. My dad was a rock singer. Did you know that?"

"No, I didn't," I lied.

"Never met him once in my whole life." I stared at him. "I could walk out that door and bump right into him, and I wouldn't recognize him."

"I don't believe you."

"So don't," he said. "Just gave me his name and said, 'So long, boy.' "

"Is that how you got named Homer?"

"Sure. His name was Homer Montague. But his group was called Little Monty and the Moonbeams. Isn't that the pits? They were famous for about forty-five minutes. Ever hear of them?"

"I don't think so."

He had started copying the science notes as we talked, and I watched fascinated as he scribbled furiously in a shorthand that must have been his own invention.

"Don't know where he is now," he said casually, as his pencil flew over the page. "Probably overdosed somewhere."

I didn't say anything, and we sat in silence until he finished the notes. I tried to absorb it all, but my mind felt like a carousel. Homer Montague sure was confusing.

When he was done, he called Henry and asked to be picked up.

While we waited on the porch, he played with Ferguson, and I almost started to laugh, seeing them face-to-face like that. They didn't really look alike. Maybe it was their personalities.

"Homer . . ."

"Yeah?"

"I'm, uh, sorry I called you a creep before."

"You called me a nut, too," he said solemnly. "Today in the media center."

"That's right . . . I did!" I said, starting to giggle. "But then you said I was crazy!"

"Right. So we're even."

"Why . . . why did you act like that at the square dance?"

He made a face. "I don't know. I just don't want to be run over, you know? Like I've gotta let you know I'm *here*." I must have looked confused, because he said, "You wouldn't understand." He was quiet for a moment and I thought he was finished, but then he said, "You know what movie stars do to regular people? Make them feel *invisible*. I'm 'the kid.' You think you'd like that? Huh? I bet you've got a name in your house, right?" Before I could think of anything to say, the long black limousine turned the corner and came slowly to a halt in front of us. "But I want you to know one thing," he said, as he got up and started down the steps.

"What's that?"

"It's true about my father." I didn't say anything. "Not once. Not once in my whole life," he shouted up at me as he walked backward to the car. Then he turned and got inside.

I stood on the porch shivering after he left. Then, as the daylight faded, I turned on the porch light for Mom and Dad and went inside.

10

"There's a big hole in my seat!" Jan cried.

"So, just move over one."

"I can't. That one's broken. Come on Cici, change with me."

I don't know why *I* had to change with her. It wasn't my fault there was a hole in her old seat. But I did anyway. We stood up and switched places, inching past Jody and Nancy. It was a good thing the movie hadn't started yet, or there would have been hissing and shouts of "sit down" from all the other people in the audience.

Who am I trying to kid? There were only fourteen of us in the Star (I had just counted), and it was almost time for the picture to start. I remember only a few years ago it would have been so crowded and noisy at a Saturday matinee, my dad would have had to go up and down the aisles making the kids shut up. But ever since that fancy new Cinema 21 opened up, we hardly had any business at all. Today we were showing two old horror movies for the price of one. I used to be so proud when we came here. My dad let us in for nothing, and I'd usher my friends down the aisle like I was a queen and this was my palace. But they didn't seem to appreciate it anymore. I practically had to beg them to come today.

The titles flashed on the screen, and I noticed the film had that grainy, spotty quality some old reels have. The sound was off a little, too. It was called *Robot Monster*, and the stars were George Nader and Claudia Barrett. The only one in the picture who looked like he knew what he was doing was Ro-Man, the monster. When it was over, the lights came on and the screen flashed a big INTERMISSION sign to the accompaniment of tinny static-filled music.

I was sitting there debating whether I wanted more popcorn, when the giggling started beside me. I nudged Nancy. "What're you guys laughing at?"

She turned around, her face suddenly serious. "Nothing," she said.

"Come on. What's the joke? I know it was an awful movie, but it wasn't that funny." I could see Jody and Jan whispering, and from the way they glanced over at me, I knew it was something I should know about.

Nancy turned to them and said, "Cut it out, you guys."

I got the queasy feeling Nancy was trying to protect me.

"Okay, what is it?" I said. They couldn't be mad at me. I didn't make the movie.

Jan nudged Jody. "I think you should tell her."

Jody shrugged. "She probably knows already. You guys are making a big thing out of nothing."

"Would you plese tell me what the nothing is that you're making a big thing out of?"

Nancy looked at me. "Benny'll probably blab it to you tomorrow anyway," she said, with a sigh, like she had just lost a battle to save my feelings. "Do you know about the Star?"

"What about it?"

"Benny says his father says it's being sold, and they're gonna put an office building here."

I felt like I had been punched in the stomach.

"That's ridiculous," I said, trying to talk calmly even though I was suddenly short of breath. "Don't you think that I would know if the theatre was being sold? This theatre has been in our family for over forty years. . . ."

"It's going to be a real nice building," Jody chimed in, as if she hadn't heard me. "A professional office building. Only doctors and dentists will be in it."

"We are a theatrical family," I said, feeling my voice beginning to crack. "What would we want with doctors' and dentists' offices?"

Jan looked impatient. "No, you don't get it. You won't own it, silly. They're gonna knock this down."

I rose unsteadily. "I'm going to get more popcorn," I said. I should have asked if they wanted some, but I couldn't. I could barely see where I was going until I reached the back where the popcorn counter was. Angie Morelli worked there on Saturdays, and she said, "Hiya Cici, what can I get ya?"

I stood there like someone in one of those zombie movies. It wasn't true. It couldn't be true. I would know, wouldn't I? Even my dad wouldn't pull a stunt like that. I'd show up one Saturday for a movie, and there'd be nothing here but a hole in the ground. This last thought made me want to laugh and cry at the same time.

I felt someone at my elbow and I looked up, hoping it wasn't one of them coming out to console me. It was Homer.

"A Mars bar," he said to Angie.

"I didn't know you were here," I said.

"I didn't get here until the lights were out. Wasn't that a great movie?"

"Very funny."

"No, I mean it. It was so terrible, it was one of the really great ones. Those are the only movies I can stand to see. The real clinkers. They must have made this one for $1.98."

"Who're you with?"

"Nobody."

"Nobody?"

Maybe I shouldn't have been surprised, but I was. It was bad enough to sit by yourself at lunchtime, but nobody went to the movies alone. Nobody. That was like announcing to the whole world that you had no friends.

"Sure," he said.

"But why here?"

"I just told you. I love disaster movies. Real disaster movies." He took a long time counting his change, then he said, "Don't let those guys get to you."

"What'd you mean?"

"I was sitting right in back of you. I heard everything."

"It's so stupid. They don't know what they're talking about," I snapped.

"Maybe they do. Let's face it, Cici, this place has gotta go."

"What are you saying?"

My voice came out high and shrill, and Paulie, the kid who takes tickets at matinee, came out and closed the door. "Keep it down, Cici, the movie's on again."

"Cripes, we're missing . . . what are we missing?" he said, straining to see the poster outside. "*The Slime People.* I can't miss that!" he said seriously, trying to get by me.

"Wait a minute!" I grabbed the sleeve of his sweater. I had never felt so awful in my life. Somehow his telling me this place was a wreck made it true. He was in the business, so he would know. He had just condemned me to oblivion. I'd be a big fat nothing all my life. "How can you say this place has gotta go! We're gonna remodel it and stay in show business!" I said.

"You're a real Looney Tune, you know that? What does this place have to do with 'show business'? Listen, I think you're wacko to like that stuff, but if you do, just . . . do. But stop acting like the Queen of the May, Cici, or you're gonna end up more alone than I am."

He went back inside and left me standing there like a dummy, with Angela Morelli's eyes boring into me. I pulled at the heavy lobby door and followed him. I had absolutely no desire to sit through *The Slime People*, but I couldn't just leave or my friends would wonder what had happened. And I didn't want to go home anyway.

"Where were you?" Nancy whispered in the darkness as I slid into my seat.

I just shrugged my shoulders and motioned her to be quiet, as if I didn't want to miss one word of this masterpiece.

I stared up at the screen vacantly, like a dead person in those murder mysteries when they haven't closed his eyes yet. Could it be true? Maybe my folks were just waiting for the right time to tell me . . . like on my birthday. . . . Surprise! You're not in show business anymore! Now, instead of visiting your family's theatre, with lights and velvet curtains and projectors and a box office, you can visit . . . what? Crandall's with its bolts of cloth? Or better yet, Jerry's Garage, where I can lose myself in gasoline fumes? If it were true, I would hate them for the rest of my life.

Whistle-stopping across the country on a blitz to publicize her new movie, Green Jungle, *Cynthia Star said "Sorry" to the folks in Schuyler when they asked her to stop at the Cinema 21 there and bring a much-needed boost to the economy of the small, dingy town. "I'm much too busy," she said. "Now if the old theatre were still there, the one my grandfather founded, the one with charm and class and dignity and heritage, I'd stop by. But I don't make personal appearances in bowling alleys—"*

Nancy let out a shriek that brought me back with a jump.

"My gosh, what's the matter?"

"Yuk, didn't you see that?" she said, pointing to the screen.

I had almost forgotten about the movie. I looked up for a moment, and then quickly looked away again.

"This is such junk," I said in disgust. "I don't know how you can even watch it."

"Sh-h-h-h" a voice said loudly in back of us.

Everyone turned around at once, and they all started giggling when they saw who it was.

"Don't tell us to shush!" I said.

"I would think Sarah Bernhardt would know how to behave in a the-a-tuh."

More giggling. I just slumped in my seat and decided to ignore him. How could you deal seriously with someone who goes to the movies alone?

It seemed like an eternity, but finally *The Slime People* slithered off the screen. As I watched the last credits fade away, I got this shivery feeling. If it were true, if it were at all possibly true, was this the last time I'd be here? Of course not. But how many more times would there be?

Nancy nudged me. "C'mon, Cici. Let's go."

I didn't see Homer anywhere. He must have left the minute the movie was over.

"Thanks Cici, that was fun," Jan said as her mom's car drew up outside. Jody started walking the other way, and she said almost the same thing.

They were being so polite, as if they felt sorry for me. That's when I began to really get scared.

11

Sheets of rain bombarded the windowpane as I pressed my forehead against it and closed my eyes. The organdy curtains felt stiff and scratchy against my cheek, but I didn't move. I knew I shouldn't be hiding up in my room like this, but things were so mixed up, so messy lately. It was as if you began to pull at a little bit of wool on the sleeve of your sweater, and all of a sudden, you ended up with a bunch of wrinkled yarn in your lap.

I could hear the sound of cupboards closing as Mom set the table in the kitchen below. I should be downstairs offering to help. The dinner had been simmering on the stove for hours, the smell greeting me as soon as I came in the door from school.

Usually I had a wonderful loose feeling on a Friday; this afternoon I felt tight as a drum. It was as if someone were tightening the wires that controlled my body, like a marionette. Tighter, tighter, soon I wouldn't be able to move at all.

I opened my eyes and shook my head. So what if Grandma was coming to dinner again? So what if every time she came to dinner lately it ended in a family argument, their voices seeping up like poisoned gas through the floor of my room. It was two against one, but Grandma would never give in. The rumors were false. She would never give up the Star.

I stayed leaning against the windowpane as the sky darkened and the streetlights came on. Then I saw the headlights, fuzzy and streaked, come down the street and stop at the curb. Grandma and Dad were home.

I pulled myself away from the window reluctantly and glanced in the mirror over my dresser before I went downstairs. I looked pale. "Washed out," Mom called it.

"Hi Grandma! Hi Dad!" I yelled, trying to sound cheerful.

"Hi sweetie," Dad said, giving me a quick hug before he went in to see Mom in the kitchen.

"Hi dear," Grandma said. "What's new with my girl?"

I shrugged my shoulders. "Nothing much. It's dullsville around here, you know that."

"Even with young Mr. Montague in school? I would think his presence would bring a rapture to your days!" she said, fluttering her eyelids.

I felt myself blush. "Oh Grandma, you don't know him. Believe me, he's no Errol Flynn," I said, remembering the name of one of Grandma's favorites.

"Well now, I didn't say he was, did I, Walt?" she

said, with a broad wink at Dad as he came back and settled in his chair. "I think I hit a nerve. Honestly, Cynthia, you don't have to marry him or nothin'!" Dad and Grandma smiled at each other and for some reason that made me even more annoyed.

"Oh God!" I said, and went into the kitchen. I was trying so hard to be calm and polite and not get into any trouble tonight. I wouldn't give anyone a reason to want to give me bad news. "Can I help?" I asked Mom.

"No dear, everything's ready." I could tell by the way she said it that she was thinking, Where have you been for the past hour?

"I've been doing homework," I said, answering the question she hadn't asked me. Then I went back out, letting the door swing shut behind me.

Sometimes I feel like I'm in a fort, completely surrounded by enemies. I'd think I was going crazy, except that Nancy feels the same way sometimes. But her house isn't as bad as mine. It couldn't be.

"Soup's on!" my mother cried gaily, placing a platter of goulash on the dining-room table.

It was the first time I noticed that the table was set in the dining room.

"Why're we being so fancy?" I asked.

My mother looked at my father, and then they both glanced over at Grandma.

"It's kind of a special occasion, Cici," Dad said. "We're gonna tell you about it."

I could feel my knees get shaky, but I slid into my seat without a word. Grandma would never do it. She'd never give in. Even if she had, we wouldn't be celebrating. She wouldn't let them gloat over it! I looked over at her, but she pretended to be busy unfolding her napkin and settling it just so on her lap.

Dad brought in a bottle of wine and poured some for the three grown-ups. I will be dignified, I thought. And aloof, and mature. If it was true, and they had done it to me, I would run away and never see any of them again, ever. Let them mourn me as if I were dead, every time they pass a newsstand and see my face; let them cry their eyes out when I chat cozily with other celebrities on news shows, and never mention their names.

"Cici, you want to take some noodles and pass them to Grandma?"

"Oh, sorry." I hastily took a spoonful and passed the bowl on.

"Is that all you're takin'? You're not dietin', are you?" Grandma said, "You're too skinny as it is."

"I'm just not that hungry."

Walter was talking about a basketball game with Dad.

"Can I, Dad? Can I go? Please? Can I, please?"

"Walter, stop whining!" I said.

The clatter of the dishes stopped as they turned and looked at me.

"Why don't you just shut up!" Walter snapped back.

"Hey, you guys, cut it out! Right now! Not tonight. We have some good news, and we want everyone in this family to be happy about it," Dad said. He was staring straight at me as he spoke. Then he cleared his throat as if he were going to announce the end of the world.

"Walt, let me," Grandma said, "let me." Then she

started clearing *her* throat. "Despite the fact," she began, in a light tone of voice, "that I am still regularly mistaken for Cheryl Tiegs, you must realize, both of you, that I'm not gettin' no younger."

"How old *are* you?" Walter interrupted.

Grandma made a face at him. "I will be thirty-three on my next birthday."

"A-a-a-a-a-h."

"Let me continue. And I think it's about time that I started takin' it easy. Also, there are two young Starretts at this table who, before you know it, are goin' to want to go to college, maybe even law school, places like that."

I couldn't believe my ears. Law school? Who was thinking of going to law school—the pigeon? He was a genuine moron. And Grandma knew I wasn't going to go to college. I wouldn't need to. . . .

"—and the Star hasn't been a money-makin' operation for years," she went on. "But the land is!"

It was happening. I looked down at my plate where the beef and the noodles and the gravy were beginning to blur together.

"Much as I hated to do it, put off doin' it for longer than I should have, I finally had to accept an excellent offer I received for the property. This means a good deal of money, so now your father can go into a business that he's wanted to be in all along. Isn't that right, Walt? Here's to the new owner of—what are you goin' to call it?"

"Starrett's Service Station," Dad said, raising his wine glass. I could hear the clinking of glasses as they all made a toast, but I didn't raise my head.

I didn't want to cry. When you're betrayed, you shouldn't cry, you should fight. But the tears came anyway. Gross and uninvited, they came.

"Cynthia luv, don't," Grandma said. Then to the others, "I told you I should have told her before, when we were alone."

"Cici." It was my mother now. "I'm sorry, hon, but we all have to grow up sometime. . . ."

I wanted to scream at her and tell them how lousy it was, talking about the Star like it was an old car they were trading in. It had always been the most important place in the world to me. And now, just because of money, they were going to end it. End everything. My face was all contorted from the effort to stop crying, and when I spoke, the words came out in gulps.

"You're not fair. It's mine, too. You just don't care!"

As I bolted from the table, I could hear Grandma saying, "Let her go, Walt. Let her go."

I slammed the door of my room and flung myself across the bed. The tears came in a deluge. I had never acted this way before. I had never felt this way before . . . so wild. Maybe I *was* going crazy. I sat up cross-legged on the bed and stared at my reflection in the mirror across the room.

Now I knew what despair felt like. Destiny's child . . . what a joke! I was still two notches above ugly, they had just stolen my birthright out from under me—and I was going bananas to boot.

Without the Star, what was I? Who would care? The fortune-teller hadn't predicted this, so maybe she was a fraud after all. My mom was right. I had to grow up. I'd go to work in Crandall's, measuring out yards of ribbon like she does. I'd have pimples and get fat and have blue veins in my legs like those women you see at the beach.

The tears came again. Maybe I'll never stop crying. Then they'd be sorry. When the ambulance came and they took me down the front steps, with all the neighbors gaping and shaking their heads—

"What a lovely young thing she was," Mrs. Reilly would say, and Mrs. Prescott would go tsk-tsk *and wipe her eyes with her handkerchief. Convulsive crying they'd call it. And they'd have no cure.*

Or maybe like in the old movies, I'd expire from melancholy. I threw myself back down on the bed and lay there staring up at the ceiling.

When I woke up it was so dark I knew it must be the middle of the night. It was still raining and the streetlights barely cast any light into my room. I slipped out of my clothes in the dark and into a nightgown and slid under the covers. It was cold. I knew I'd feel awful in the morning, maybe even a bit guilty. And hungry. Definitely. Very, *very* hungry.

12

When I woke up, the sun was streaming in the window and the alarm clock was making faces at me. Eight-thirty—and I had promised Nancy I'd be at the eighth-grade carwash by nine. I didn't feel as if I had slept at all. Or if I had, it was a sleep filled with bad dreams. Bad dreams that were *real*, just waiting for me to get up and face them.

I swung my legs over the side of the bed and stretched. Maybe I could sneak out without seeing anybody. I'd love to do that . . . and keep doing it for about five years. By then I'd be old enough to leave home.

But first I had to get some food. I was absolutely famished.

I bounded down the stairs, tucking my shirt into my jeans as I reached the bottom step. Maybe I'd just grab a roll. I could hear a buzz saw outside, so I knew Dad was working in the yard. If I could just get through the kitchen . . . but the figure sitting bent over a coffee mug stopped me. Was it my imagination, or was she suddenly old?

"Gram . . . I didn't know you were here."

"Of course you didn't. You were sleepin'. You were sleepin' when I went up to talk to you last night, too. So I came over early 'cause I wanted to catch you before you went runnin' off somewhere."

"Gram, I have to run. I promised Nancy I'd be at the carwash before nine, and it's nine already."

She looked up at me and her eyes looked just like they do in her pictures: round and blue and sad.

"You're really mad at me, aren't you, Cynthia? You don't understand at all, do you?"

I could feel myself tighten up inside, like there was a rock at my core, and it was just going to get bigger and bigger. "I understand all right," I wanted to say, "but I don't have to like it!"

"Sure I do, Gram. It's okay. I just got a little upset. It was such a shock, you know."

"Honest, Cynthia?" she said, with a note of pleading in her voice that I had never heard before. It made her seem old and helpless, and I hated it.

"Of course, Gram, don't be silly. Like Mom says, I've gotta grow up. Listen, I've really gotta run." I bent over and gave her a hug. "Don't forget to bring your car through the wash today. It's for a good cause," I said, as I bounded out the door and down the steps. I let the door slam noisily behind me, just like always. Just like nothing had changed. I realized halfway down the street that I had forgotten my roll, but I was very pleased with myself anyway. I had just given a magnificent performance.

I don't know why I told Nancy I'd work at the eighth-grade carwash. Of all the dumb ways to waste a Saturday.

Correction: I *do* know why I said I'd do it. Ever since we went on that hike, those things Homer said had been bothering me. I do *so* do things with my friends! I'd show them.

Being a good friend, and not wanting to show any favoritism, Nancy had given me the worst job on the whole carwash line: slosher. A slosher is someone who dips this huge sponge into the soapy water and lathers up the car. The people after the slosher have fun: They get to use the hose. The people after that have fun: They get to shine up the cars. The people at the gate have the most fun of all: They get to play store and take the money. But all sloshers do is get wet. The dirty water runs down your arms and onto your clothes.

"Look," she said, when I objected, "I put you with David Petersen."

"Big deal. You know I don't like David Petersen anymore. I haven't liked David Petersen ever since that day I wore orange culottes to school, and he told Amy Goldberg I looked like a cantaloupe."

"Boy, do you bear a grudge. That was in fifth grade."

"A cantaloupe's a cantaloupe, Nancy. Some things never change."

"Please, Cici? If I can't count on you, who can I count on? What are friends for? If I make anybody else a slosher, I've made an enemy for life!"

"Oh. Since you put it that way . . ."

So I worked as a slosher. By eleven o'clock my arm felt like one huge soggy sponge, and my stomach was growling so loudly you could hear it over the rumble of the car engines.

I looked around for someone who might want to change places with me. Spotting a new girl taking tickets halfway down the entrance ramp, I dropped my sponge in the bucket and said, "I'll be right back" to David. I ran up to her planning how official I could sound. I'd say, "This is the way it's done at Schuyler: If you're dry as a bone and having a great time taking tickets, and a walking wet mop comes over to you and offers to switch, you jump at the chance."

"Joan," I said, cheer ringing from every word, "you want to switch? I'll take tickets, and you can be a slosh—on the soap committee."

She looked me up and down slowly, and I think I know now how the Loch Ness monster feels when he pokes his head out of the water every once in a while. No wonder he keeps diving back into the sea. It's enough to hurt anybody's feelings.

"Uh, thanks," she said, "but I don't think so."

"Are you sure?" I asked weakly, trying to look pitiful and gain some sympathy.

"Nope! Whoops, we're getting a backup here," she said. "Sorry, sir! That'll be two dollars."

I ran back to the slosher station and apologized to David, who was in a big sulk because I had left him on his own to handle the steady stream of cars that was snaking down the driveway. That was another reason, I remember, that I didn't like David Petersen anymore—he was always sulking.

I continued sloshing for another half hour, getting more miserable by the minute. All around me, kids seemed to be enjoying themselves, but I felt as removed from it all as if I were visiting earth from another planet. And in a way that was it: My personal world had changed, probably forever. I felt the tears come to my eyes a couple of times, and I had to fight them back and try not to think about it. I hadn't said anything to Nancy yet. Maybe they all knew about it anyway. Nancy would be sympathetic, I was sure of that. But she'd say something dumb like, "Hey, maybe you can still try out for the cheerleading squad!" and I'd have to punch her.

I heard some shouts and laughter from the kids shining up cars on the end of the line, and I looked over and saw Homer standing there trying to look like one of the gang. Somehow he always stood out, as if he were all alone, even when he wasn't.

I sneezed and realized suddenly that I was shivering. It would serve them right if I got pneumonia.

"Hey David, I've got to get some time off. Who's supposed to relieve us?"

"I dunno. But I get relieved first. I only have to work till twelve."

"Who says?"

"Nancy."

"Nancy?" The sponge dropped into the bucket making a splash that soaked the last dry spot on my body. "I'll be right back," I said to David, again.

Nancy had joined the group standing at the far end of the parking lot. When they saw me, everybody started to laugh.

"God, Cici, how do you get yourself into such a mess? You're drenched!" Nancy said.

"Of course I am," I said. "So will you be, after you spend the rest of the afternoon over there."

A flicker of fear crossed her face. "I . . . I can't work, Cici. I'm co-chairperson. You know that!"

"Well, sorry, Princess Diana, but somebody's working for me. You promised David Petersen he could quit at twelve."

"Oh, well, that's because he has to go to the dentist. It's an emergency."

"Well, you'll have an emergency at the dentist, too, if you don't get somebody to relieve me. I've gotta get out of these clothes. And I've gotta eat, Nancy. I'm starving. I haven't eaten in almost twenty-four hours!" The magnitude of that statement made me weak.

Out of the corner of my eye, I saw Homer leaning against a parked car, but I just ignored him. The one person in this entire world I really didn't want to talk to was him. He'd start some of his double-talk again, and I'd end up feeling sorry for him—somebody who had everything. Today the only person I wanted to feel sorry for was Cici Starrett.

"Cici, you look like you just had a blind date with Moby Dick!" Joey Steinberg said, and everybody started laughing again.

I could feel myself ready to explode. All I wanted to do was get out of there. "C'mon Nancy, I don't feel so good. You've got to get somebody to relieve me."

"Gee Cici, I'm sorry. Okay, I'll get somebody. But I don't know who . . ."

"I'll relieve you."

I glanced over to where he was slouched against the car. Of all the people I expected to rescue me, he was last on the list. I shrugged. "Fine," I said, and I started back to where I had been working. I could hear Nancy behind me letting out a sigh of relief.

"Gee, that's great of you. Isn't that great?" she asked the others. I thought for a moment they were going to give him a round of applause.

I walked back to the sloshing station in silence. I could hear him right behind me, but I pretended not to notice. This was a perfect example of life's inequity. I could slosh until my arm fell off and I wouldn't even get a "thank you." But just be somebody (or somebody's son), and every time you burp they give you a ticker-tape parade!

I introduced him to Billy Owens, David's replacement.

"I'll be back as soon as I can," I said.

"You don't have to come back."

"What do you mean? You don't want to stay here."

"Why not? I got no plans. You're feeling lousy, so stay home."

"I'm not feeling lousy!" I said, stepping out of the way as a big green station wagon rolled up. I watched him start to work. Only a few drops got on his sleeve, but he'd get soaked like everybody else. No matter who he was, he wasn't waterproof.

"Could have fooled me," he said, not looking up from the car. "Your grandmother did a real smart thing, Cici. That's business. You gotta grow up and realize that, and stop being such a baby."

I started to say something, but he had knocked the wind out of me. I felt the way I did the first time I'd heard about it, from Nancy, that day in the Star. If he knew, everybody knew, and they were probably all laughing at me.

"I really think you have your nerve," I said, lowering my voice. "You have everything, and all you do is complain and act crazy. You have no idea what it's like to be just an ordinary person. That theatre made me *special*."

I turned and fled, running out of the parking lot and down the hill, the cold wind biting my face. "His real name is *Homer*," I yelled at the top of my lungs. But nobody heard, and only the wind answered.

13

I thought I was handling it pretty well. Since that first night, I hadn't yelled, cried, stamped my feet, bitten anyone, or in any other way shown that my hopes had been dashed to the ground, my world shattered, and my future snatched right out of my hands.

But obviously they suspected. I heard them whispering constantly. One day I came in from school, and Grandma and Mom were in the kitchen.

"It's my fault, Maureen," Grandma was saying. "I know that now. Thing is, if I had it to do over again, I'm sure I'd do the very same thing. I'm that selfish."

Grandma's voice shook when she spoke, and I couldn't bear to hear it. She had let them turn her into a little old lady almost overnight.

Dad, on the other hand, went around *whistling*. I

came home from the library one night, and he was stretched out with his feet up on the ottoman, all ready to doze off. He looked so happy and contented, I couldn't help feeling guilty. Why couldn't I be happy for him? Part of me said, "Look, Cici, he's hated managing the Star for ten years. Now he can have his own business, doing something he's really good at. He deserves that!" But the other part of me said, "Sure, but that means it's *my* turn to have a miserable ten years. By that time I'll be twenty-three, and life will have passed me by." It was like some grotesque fairy tale. Everybody gets a chance to be happy for ten years—and wouldn't you know it—my ten years were already up. I don't even remember most of them.

One night when we were all sitting around after dinner, Mom said, "Cici, you're so quiet. What are you thinking?"

I hesitated a moment. Should I tell them what I was *really* thinking?

"I'm thinking I've never seen all of you so happy," I said. "Really. I'm so glad. Dad's happy. Grandma's happy. You're happy. Where's the pigeon? I'll bet he's absolutely hysterical!"

I have no idea where I suddenly got off sounding like an old Joan Crawford movie.

My mother looked like she had just been forced to swallow an entire prune Danish. Whole.

"Cynthia, what's come over you? I won't have a child of mine talking like that!"

"Oh, all of a sudden, I'm a child again. I thought

you wanted me to grow up? Isn't that what you said? Be sensible. Put on a sturdy pair of loafers and go to work in Crandall's for the rest of my life!"

I was beginning to scare myself. Did you ever see a puppy when he barks for the first time, and then he jumps and looks around to see who made the noise? That's what I felt like.

"Go to your room," my father said quietly.

I went to my room, all right. I ran up those stairs so fast I almost tripped. I had never felt so out of control. I was so mixed up. It was as if everything had been a dream and now I woke up, and I didn't know who I was or how things were going to turn out. Before I'd always been so *sure*.

I slammed the door and hurled myself onto the bed. I lay there trembling. I didn't cry. I hadn't really cried since the night I found out about the sale.

There was a knock on the door, and before I could say "Come in" or "Go away" the door opened, and my mother was standing there with her hand on the doorknob. She didn't say anything and neither did I.

I sat up and, lacking any great purpose in life, began pulling at the chenille in the bedspread. I could feel my throat tightening up. "You don't understand," I said finally.

My mother closed the door behind her and sat down next to me. "What makes you so sure of that?"

I let out a big sigh and looked straight into my mother's eyes. They were still very blue and pretty, but the skin around them had little wrinkles in it.

"You don't like show business or anything like that."

"But don't you see, that isn't what this is all about! What does that crumbling old wreck of a building have to do with show business?"

Why did people keep asking me that? I could feel tears forcing themselves to the surface. "That's what I mean! It's just an old building to you. But that's not what it is to me. That's not what it used to be to Grandma. I don't know how she could have changed so much."

"Maybe she hasn't changed, Cici. Don't you see? Maybe other things have changed. Like the Star. Maybe that's what's changed, and Grandma is the same as she's always been." I wiped my nose on a corner of the bedspread, and I saw my mother make a face but she didn't say anything. "Cici, if you want to be in show business, that old building shouldn't stand in your way, whether it's still standing or not! I know you think your father and I are so dull we couldn't possibly understand"—I started to protest, but she went on—"Not everybody likes that kind of life. If you think a Gillian Dawn is a person to admire, fine." She got up and folded my robe, laying it carefully on the chair. "I just wish you'd open yourself up a little. You've got so many more options than I did. Don't be so—so *narrowminded*." She screwed up her face. "That's not really the word I was looking for, but it'll have to do. Now, I want you to make peace with your grandmother. I haven't agreed with her nonsense about you all these years, but she's your grandmother and you have no right to make her suffer so. So I'll expect you back downstairs in five minutes, and when you get there, you offer to walk her home." She started to leave and then she turned back. "And by the way, Cici. In order to be hired by Crandall's, you have to know everything there is to know about sewing, and fabrics, and good workmanship. *You* wouldn't make it. Come to think of it, neither would Gillian Dawn." And she slammed my door.

It was a clear, cold night with lots of stars, a sliver of moon, and just enough frost in the air to make you feel that winter would be beautiful when it came. We walked along slowly, with me taking smaller steps so Grandma wouldn't have to rush. She seemed so different suddenly, like all the electricity had drained out of her, and now she was just like everybody else's grandmother: a nice-looking, plain old lady with gray hair and glasses. Tall, but stooped over. Gone were the cape and the horse and the grand adventure. I tried to keep a conversation going, but it was hard.

"Do you think the Willoughbys are going to sell? Mom says they are. They're going to retire and move to Florida."

"Hmm. Could be."

"If they sell, it would be nice if kids my age moved in. Or maybe little kids that I could baby-sit for. I'd be rich."

"That would be nice."

We got to her door, and I waited while she took out her key. After she unlocked the door, she put the key back in her handbag and closed it firmly. Then she turned to me with a sigh. "I don't suppose you want to come in? Maybe have some hot chocolate?"

I nodded. "Sure."

I went into the parlor while Grandma went through to the kitchen and put some water on to boil. I stood in the middle of the room, almost as if I were a stranger visiting for the first time, waiting to be invited to stay. My glance fell on the round table with the shawl draped over it. The pictures of Dad and Grandpa, and Walter and me, Mom and Dad on their wedding day— The pictures from Hollywood were gone.

I went over and looked carefully. It was like they had vanished into thin air. They were such a fixture in this room, in my memories, that I stood touching one picture after another, feeling sure that they were there somewhere. But they were really and truly gone.

I heard Grandma come into the room, and I turned around and stared at her.

"Where are they?"

"Hmm? What, dear?" she said, like a befuddled old lady who didn't understand what I was saying.

"The pictures! What did you do with them?"

"Oh. I put them away."

"But—*why?*"

She looked at me a moment, blinking her eyes behind her glasses as if trying to think of what she could answer. She settled herself into a chair before she spoke.

"Should have done it years ago, Cynthia. They were so old. You can't live in the past, for goodness' sake. It was all foolishness. Now those pictures, those are the memories I want to keep," she said firmly, gesturing to the pictures of the family.

I sank down on the couch where I always sat,

nudging Snowball over as I did. The cat got up and stretched. Then she came over and settled down next to me again, covering me with angora as she did.

"You really don't care anymore, do you? How could you have changed so much?"

She spread her hands out on her lap and smoothed her dress as if it were a tablecloth and she were setting a place for dinner.

"I care, Cynthia. I care. But what has that got to do with"—and she waved her hand in the direction of the table where the pictures used to sit. "You can't spend your whole life relivin' things that happened when you were twenty-one. No, I've been doin' a lot of thinkin' lately, Cynthia. And I haven't been fair. Not to your father, and most of all, not to you."

"I don't know what you mean. Up to now you've always been fair to me. It's now that you're not being fair."

Grandma shook her head vigorously. "No, no, you don't understand!" she said vehemently, sounding for a brief moment as she used to. The kettle split the air with its piercing whistle. "I'll be right back," she said, and she got up and hurried into the kitchen.

She was back in a moment, handing me a mug of hot chocolate and setting her teacup down on the table next to her chair. Arranging herself comfortably again, she said, "Listen to me, Cynthia, and listen good. When I first laid eyes on you, when you were first born, I thought you were the prettiest thing I'd ever seen. And you got more so. Why when you were two years old, people used to stop me on the street when I took you for a walk. You looked—how can I say it—*special*. And that's when I took it into my head that you were my second chance. I'll admit, I was a bit disappointed at the way things turned out for me. Oh, your grandpa was a good man, and we were happy enough. But I always had this feelin' I had missed somethin'. So I spent half my time dreamin' about what used to be or could have been, and the other half plannin' how wonderful it was gonna be for you. Never mind whether it was right for you or not. That never entered my head. It was like you was Snowball there, just put here to give me comfort and pleasure." She stopped and lifted the teacup to her lips. I noticed her hand trembling.

"It's all right, Gram. Don't get upset. I'm sorry. I didn't mean to—"

She looked at me, and her voice was laced with anger. "Don't you be sorry, Cynthia Ann Starrett. It's me that's sorry. I'm just a foolish old woman, and I've made trouble for everyone. How your mother's put up with me, God only knows."

"That's not true! You're not foolish." I jumped up and pointed to the table frantically. "That was something to be proud of. You were beautiful and did things that not many people get to do. Don't let Mom and Dad make you feel guilty. You didn't do anything to me. If I wasn't like you, if I didn't want to be a star, I wouldn't have paid any attention, would I?"

She took another sip of her tea. Then another. Then slowly she looked at me and cocked her head to the side in a gesture so familiar it made me ache. She didn't smile exactly, but her face brightened.

"I'm sorry I've been so mean about the Star," I said. "I guess it meant something special to me, as if it were a sign of something."

"You don't need no signs, Cynthia. You don't need me or nothin' but yourself. You know I always said you was destiny's ch—" She caught herself then, and we both started to laugh.

"Please put the pictures back, Gram."

"Does it mean so much to you?"

I nodded. I couldn't explain it to her exactly, but her putting the pictures away was like she was preparing to die. And I could feel myself crumble at the thought.

We finished our tea and cocoa, and I washed and dried the cups before I left.

14

"Those movie people are getting set to quit Schuyler," my dad said, rattling the evening paper as he turned the page.

Grandma glanced over to me. "Oh?" she said innocently. "When does it say they'll be gone?"

"Halloween. That's the last day of filming. *That's* for publicity purposes," he said knowingly, " 'cause it's a horror flick."

"Halloween. That's a week from tomorrow, isn't it, Cynthia?" Grandma asked.

"Yep." I nodded. I looked over at Grandma and as our eyes met, we smiled at each other. Things had been getting better and better between us ever since that night at her house. It wasn't the same exactly, but I was beginning to realize that things never stay the same. Just like people don't stay the same. Grandma wasn't exactly the way she used to be, but she wasn't acting so old and frail anymore. And she had put the pictures back on the table.

It was while I was clearing the table after dinner that I got my idea. Gillian Dawn had said—what was it she had said exactly? *Maybe you can bring Granny around to the set sometime.* If I didn't do it soon, I wouldn't have another chance. They'd be leaving in a week, and it would all be gone forever.

I tossed the idea of visiting the set into the back of my mind for a few days. After all, it was still off limits to the public, and I didn't need any more humiliation.

Then, one day after English class, destiny took me by the hand and led me to the water fountain.

"Hi," I said cheerfully, when he stood up after taking a drink.

He looked at me warily, like I wasn't to be trusted. "Hi."

It was an encouraging sign, I figured, that he hadn't just said "What?"

"I read in the paper that the movie's almost finished. They're wrapping it up on Halloween, right?" He nodded. "Does that mean you'll be leaving Schuyler?" I tried to make my eyes mist up, but it wasn't any use. I just wasn't that talented. Again he nodded. "Well, say, uh, your mom . . . Gillian Dawn?" He nodded to let me know he knew who I was talking about. "She invited me to bring my grandmother over to the set. Remember, that night at your house?"

"So?"

"Well," I said, beginning to get cold feet, "how do I get in? I mean, I don't want to bring my grandmother all the way over there and end up standing at those big iron bars again."

"When do you want to come?"

"Oh," I said, "anytime. Tomorrow?"

"Okay. Come over after school. I'll meet you at the front entrance at three-thirty."

"Gee, thanks," I said. It had gone easier than I had expected. I turned to go, but he put his hand on my arm.

"How come you're bringing your grandmother over to the set?"

"Well, because, you know how my grandmother is. I just thought she'd enjoy it."

"Oh."

"Why else would I?"

"I don't know. I was just wondering. I thought you weren't getting along with your grandmother since she sold the movie house."

"Oh, that," I said. "We made up. I understand now. I really do."

I pulled away from him and hurried down the hall, pretending I had a class to get to. But I ducked into the girls' room instead. Why did he make me feel so guilty? Everything I had told him was true. We had made up. I wasn't mad at Grandma anymore. And in a way I *did* understand. But I still wanted to be somebody, and Gillian Dawn was more important to me than ever. I hoped Grandma would enjoy meeting her. But more than that, *I* had to see her again.

I brushed my hair off my face with my hand and went back into the hall. I had a right to do what I needed to do, and if Homer Montague didn't like it, that was too bad.

121

Grandma's reaction when I told her where we were going was even better than I had expected.

"Oh my, what'll I wear? What'll I wear? Oh Cynthia, you should have given me more notice! I wonder, no, I don't suppose none of the old gang from Warners would be around. Must be all retired by now. Or maybe dead. Who's makin' this movie anyways? They have all these young kids makin' movies now, none of those good studio people—"

Grandma had gone into her bedroom and opened the closet door. She fingered her dresses gingerly. I saw her touch the spangled housedress, and my heart sank. She wouldn't— But she passed it by, and when she came to a plain silk shirtwaist, I said, "We're not going to get dressed up, Gram. Why don't you wear the blue dress?"

"You think so? That is my newest, just got it at Easter."

"And it brings out the blue in your eyes," I said, mighty pleased with myself for thinking to say that. Grandma had always gotten compliments on her blue eyes.

"Did Gillian Dawn really ask you to bring me? Honest, Cynthia, you can tell me the truth."

"Honest, Gram. She's probably mad that I haven't brought you over sooner. She told me ages ago. Now you get your beauty sleep, and we'll go over tomorrow after I get home from school, okay?"

It was nice arriving at the gate in a car this time, instead of trudging all the way up the hill on foot. When we drove along the bumpy road to the main gate, there was Homer, standing inside waiting for us. We started to get out, but he called for us to wait, then he unlocked the gates and flung them open, ushering us through with an exaggerated sweep of his arm.

Grandma started up the car again and made a sharp right-hand turn, and we were through and onto the Beaumont estate. Homer climbed in the back seat after relocking the gates, and we proceeded slowly down the driveway, seeing nothing at first but an archway of red and gold trees. Then it appeared again, just as it had that first time I was here, the Beaumont mansion looming suddenly into view. Homer told Grandma where to park, and then we got out just as one of the sound men motioned us to be silent.

We stood awkwardly in a clump of trees, and it was as it had been before: wires strung everywhere; large, complicated-looking machines; cameras on dollies that allowed them to be moved around. One man was on a platform way up in the trees. I couldn't even imagine what his job was. And then I realized—it was supposed to be raining, and suddenly it was. It came down from the "sky" in torrents just as the door of the mansion flew open and Gillian Dawn came running out in hysterics. She stood screaming, letting herself get drenched by the waterfall from above. Then a second character, a young man, came out behind her. He looked menacing at first, but when he came up and grabbed her shoulder, she whirled around and threw herself into his arms. It sure looked silly watching it from this angle.

"Cut," someone ordered.

"That's it," a man nearby said to his companion. "Man, I can't wait to get out of here. Been a long day."

I turned to Homer. "It's weird. I know when this is all finished, I'll be sitting in a movie theatre and believing the whole thing. But it looks so silly now."

"I think it's silly when I see it in a movie theatre."

"That's what it's all about, Cynthia," Grandma said. "There's all sorts of jobs on a movie set. Some of them maybe don't seem so important, but they are, even the little ones. Because when you put them all together, you got yourself a movie!"

"Right, Gram," I said, not really listening, because Gillian Dawn had wrapped her head in a towel and Homer was nudging us forward.

"If you want to see my mom you better see her now," he said.

We went up to her slowly, and when she turned and saw us, there was an instant when she didn't seem to remember me, and my heart sank. But then she flashed a big smile and held out her hand.

"Well, hi there, look who's here. My competition!" I could feel myself blush, but I was pleased she had said that. That meant she really and truly remembered me.

"Miss Dawn, I'd like you to meet my grandmother," I said, "Polly Starrett."

Gillian Dawn offered her hand to Grandma and smiled quickly. Then she turned back to me. "I thought I told you to call me Gillie."

"I'm sorry."

Her maid came over, and together they turned and started back to the trailer. She stopped after she had gone a few feet and motioned me to follow. "Come on, squirt, you can come, too." I followed ecstatically.

The dressing room looked the same as before, and I pressed myself into a corner while Gillian Dawn went behind a screen to change. She and Marie kept up a steady stream of conversation.

"Tell them I won't do the interview if that barracuda is writing it. She tore me up into little pieces last time."

"But Bob wants you to do it."

"Tell Bob *he* can do it. I don't need it. Let her paw over *his* psyche with those claws of hers. See how he likes it. Oh, and Marie, remind me to tell Natalie to postpone the London trip. I'm too beat. I'm going to take a few weeks off, maybe go to the Islands. Excuse me, sweetie," she said, coming out from behind the screen and settling herself at the table. I went and sat on the other side of the room and continued to listen raptly to their chatter.

"What about Homer?" Marie asked.

"Check with Natalie. He can go away to school again or whatever."

People came in and went out, asking questions, checking details, telling her bits of news, but no one seemed to notice I was in the room. Even Marie never once let on, by a blink or a nod of her head, that I was there.

Something Homer had told me popped into my head: Movie stars make regular people feel invisible. That's what I felt like, invisible. I didn't like it. An empty, lonely feeling swept over me, and then right behind it, a feeling of panic. Grandma! Where was she? I had traipsed in here and left her all alone out there. Oh, Cynthia Starrett, I thought, you're just *mean* enough to be a big star!

I jumped up. "I have to go," I said.

Gillian Dawn was applying mascara, and she didn't move her hand from her lashes as she mumbled, "So long." Well, I thought, at least she didn't call me kid.

I went back onto the set, and it was quieter now. Most of the people had gone, but the wires and the booms and the cameras were still there. I saw Grandma right away. She was standing with Homer over in the corner, with her back to me.

"Gram," I called out as I came up to them, "I'm sorry I took so long. . . ."

When she turned around, I could see that she had been crying, and my heart flipped over. Oh gosh, what had I done? I had been so dazzled by Gillian Dawn, Grandma hadn't even had a chance to speak to her. "Oh Gram," I said, "I'm so sorry—"

But as I came over to her, she smiled and I realized they were happy tears, the way people look at weddings.

"Oh Cynthia, I've had the grandest time." I glanced at Homer, but he looked away. "It was just like the old days! There was a grip here who just finished doing a TV movie with an actor I remember from *Dark Victory*. He's getting on now, but Charlie, that's the grip's name, said he's as good as ever. And you know that little man with the accent in the blue shirt?" I must have looked confused, because she said, "Right over *there*," pointing to where some men were finishing up. "Well, he has the same job your grandpa had. But what it took your grandfather two hours to do, he does in twenty-five minutes! *Really!*" she added, as if I wouldn't be able to believe such a thing.

We had started walking over to the car as we talked, and I tried to sort out all the confused feelings I had. I looked over at Homer. Somehow I thought he could help, but he didn't seem to want to look at me.

As we reached the car, Gillian Dawn came out of the camper with Marie and called over to Homer.

"I've got to go," he said to Grandma.

"Look," I said desperately, "there's Gillian Dawn, Gram. Maybe we can walk her to her limousine."

Grandma looked at me with a puzzled expression on her face as she lowered herself into the driver's seat of the car. "Now, Cynthia Ann," she said, "why on earth would we want to do that?"

15

Grandma talked nonstop all the way home in the car.

"Oh, when I saw that little Giorgio man workin' that lift, I can't tell you the chills that went up my spine. It was like I was back at Warners again. All the people bustlin' around. Only this set was so quiet—"

"Grandma, that was a stop sign!"

"I know, dear. Of course, they always used to say the soundstage took its personality from the star. Now, when Jane Wyman or Myrna Loy . . ."

"Grandma! Didn't you see that truck?"

"Of course I did, dear. It was very nice. They were always so *refined*. Now, Carole Lombard, God rest her soul, she was a different story—"

She was as wacky as I'd ever seen her. Maybe more so. It was as if she had gotten an injection of something back there. But I couldn't understand it. I had come away feeling, well, invisible. There was that word again. Hadn't she noticed that Gillian Dawn had hardly spoken to her? She had spent all her time with the crew, the ordinary people who worked behind the scenes. How could she think working a lift was exciting? It was like running a garage, for goodness' sake.

When we pulled up at my door, I went into the house feeling more confused than I'd ever felt before. It was very clear that Grandma hadn't really cared about meeting Gillian Dawn. All she cared about was being on a movie set again. That's where she had been young and happy and had done something that she loved to do. *That* was the magic for Grandma. I wondered if she knew.

The next few days went by in slow motion, and then it was the day before Halloween. It used to be my favorite holiday, but now it makes me feel sad. We don't go trick-or-treating anymore, and everyone pretends we don't care, that it's kid stuff and too boring. But secretly we all miss it.

Saturday night there's a Halloween dance, and we'll all go dressed as bums to show how cool we are. I'd just love to go as a witch. Or better yet, a fairy princess.

"You always get too gruesome," Jody said to Nancy. "We can't use stuff like that."

"What are you guys talking about?" I asked, throwing my brown bag on the lunch table and collapsing into a chair.

"Nothing much. It's just very hard being part of a decorating team with somebody who wants to be a veterinarian," Jody said.

"What?"

Nancy raised her eyebrows to show that they just didn't understand her.

"She gets so—so—"

"Clinical. I think that's the word you're searching for," Jan threw in.

"Yeah, that's it," Jody said. "Nancy's idea of decorating the gym for Halloween is having real skeletons and rotting bones."

"How about some real live worms wriggling all over the floor?" Jan added.

"Cut it out! I didn't say that. I just think we should do something besides orange plastic pumpkins."

"Well, pumpkins don't come in any other colors," I said, trying to be helpful.

She glared at me. "Thanks a lot. You don't even know what we're talking about."

I flinched a little and finished eating my sandwich in silence.

"C'mon guys, we've got time before the bell, let's go to the gym. I'll show you what I mean!" Nancy said.

"This I've gotta see," Jody said, rolling her eyeballs at me.

The three of them got up, threw away their lunch wrappings, and headed for the gym. I sat there feeling like one of the great unwashed. They didn't even ask me to go along and watch.

I got up and went outside. It was getting really cold. It was always freezing on Halloween. Even if the rest of the week was glorious Indian summer, there was a rule somewhere, I was sure of it, that the temperature had to drop on October 31 so kids had a choice: Either you covered up your costume with a parka, or you got pneumonia.

Some kids were tossing a football around out on the field, and some girls I didn't know very well were sitting on the stone bench by the entrance to the school. I looked over to the side, and sure enough, there was Homer, sitting on the hill by himself with a book propped up in front of him.

I shivered and put my hands in my pockets. Maybe I'd go back inside and go to the girls' room. There was always somebody in there. Then I remembered how tomorrow would be Homer's last day in school, and I wondered if he intended to come to the dance. I walked over to where he was sitting.

I stood for a minute, looking down over his shoulder. He was reading *Catcher in the Rye*. If he knew I was there, he didn't show it. After a minute or two, I lowered myself onto the grass next to him. I could feel the cold, damp earth even through my corduroy pants.

"What are you reading?" I asked.

He held the book's cover up to me so I could see. Then he went on reading.

"I, uh, wanted to thank you for taking my grandmother and me over to the set the other day. She really got a kick out of it."

"Oh really?" he said.

"Yeah, *really*."

"Gee, it didn't seem to me she could've gotten much of a kick out of one handshake. I figure she saw my mom for about, oh, thirty seconds." He said all this without lifting his eyes from the book. He could have been *reading* it.

I could feel myself flush. "Well, you know, your mom is so busy. I mean, what Grandma really enjoyed was looking around the set and seeing all those people who work there. They were like the people she used to know."

For the first time, he turned and stared at me. "Cici, how could she have enjoyed talking to those people? They're so ordinary," he said.

He was being mean and sarcastic, and for a moment I wanted to spit at him and run away. Let him take that home from Schuyler as a souvenir! But inside me I knew he was right. I felt as if a fog lens had been lifted and I was seeing things clearly for the first time. Not everything in the whole world. Not the meaning of life and heavy stuff like that. But something about being famous and not being famous.

"I felt invisible the other day," I said finally. He didn't answer me, but I could see something in his face relax, and it made me feel a little better. "I think I know maybe how you feel sometimes." He turned and glared at me again, as if I had just made a ridiculous statement. How could I know what he went through day in and day out? "I know it wasn't as bad for me as it must be for you. I just want to say—I'm sorry."

He didn't say anything, so I got up to leave. "And, I'm sorry," I added, "that we didn't get a chance to be better friends."

He didn't say anything, so I turned and began to walk away.

"Cici?" he called after me. I whirled around. "You're lucky. Damn lucky" was all he said.

"Come to the dance on Saturday!" The way I said it, it sounded like an order.

"And miss the wrap party on the set?" he asked, with a note of horror in his voice.

"Yeah," I said, feeling myself smile, "let them miss you!"

And I waved and ran back into the school.

It was five minutes until the bell, but I went by the gym anyway. Jody and Nancy were having a heated discussion under the basketball hoop.

I went over to where they were standing. "Hi," I said.

"Hi," they both said impatiently, as if they didn't have time for me.

"Black streamers will make it look like President Lincoln's funeral procession," Jody was saying.

"And orange streamers will make it look like Popsicle City."

"How about," I interrupted, "if you took both colors, but not streamers, something else"—my mind worked frantically—"uh, *hair ribbons*—no—*shoelaces*, that's it! Millions and millions of shoelaces—"

The warning bell rang and they turned and started out of the gym.

"Who does she think she is, all of a sudden," Jody said, glancing over her shoulder at me. "An interior decorator?"

"Hey," I said, hurrying to catch up with them, "you know, that's not a bad idea!"

16

"Cynthia Star, you've outdone yourself!" the lady of the house gushed, throwing out her arms to encompass the small sitting room. "This room, all the rooms, are truly magnificent. How can we ever thank you?"

"It was my privilege," I said humbly. "I must admit that a house of this size was a bit overwhelming at first. But it did turn out rather nice, didn't it?"

"It's elegant!"

"But cozy," I reminded her.

"Exactly. I don't know any other designer who could have pulled it off. No wonder you've risen to the top at such a tender age."

I felt myself blushing at the extravagant praise. "That's very kind of you. But I must be going now. I have a plane to catch."

"Not London again?"

"I'm afraid so."

"I guess a castle that size would keep you busy. But I'm

so sorry you won't get a chance to meet my husband. He wanted to thank you personally."

"That's very kind of him, but I have to run."

"Are you sure? I know the Cabinet meeting will be over any moment—"

Pacer

BOOKS FOR YOUNG ADULTS

__ **THE ADVENTURES OF A TWO-MINUTE WEREWOLF**
 by Gene DeWeese   21082-2/$2.25
When Walt finds himself turning into a werewolf, one two-minute transformation turns into a lifetime of hair-raising fun!

__ **FIRST THE GOOD NEWS**
 by Judie Angell   21156-X/$2.25
Determined to win the school newspaper contest, ninth-grader Annabelle Goobitz concocts a scheme to interview a TV star—with hilarious results!

__ **MEMO: TO MYSELF WHEN I HAVE A TEENAGE KID**
 by Carol Snyder   08906-1/$2.50
Thirteen-year-old Karen is sure her mom will never understand her—until she reads a diary that changes her mind...

__ **MEGAN'S BEAT**
 by Lou Willett Stanek   08416-7/$2.50
Megan never dreamed that writing a teen gossip column would win her so many friends from the city—or cost her so many from the farm!